Contents

DRACULA

Dramatis Personae

Count Dracula

Jonathan Harker

Mina Murray / Harker

Jonathan's fiancée / wife

Lucy Westenra

Friend of Mina Murray

Arthur Holmwood

(Later, Lord Godalming)

Lucy's fiancé

Dr. John "Jack" Seward

Friend of Arthur Holmwood

Quincey Morris

American friend of Arthur Holmwood

Renfield

Dr. Seward's patient

Dr. Abraham Van Helsing

Professor and friend of Dr. Seward

Prologue

How these papers have been placed in sequence will be made manifest in the reading of them. All needless matters have been eliminated, so that a history almost at variance with the possibilities of latter-day belief may stand forth as simple fact. There is throughout no statement of past things wherein memory may err, for all the records chosen are exactly contemporary, given from the standpoints and within the range of knowledge of those who made them.

CHAPTER ONE

Jonathan Harker's Journal
3 May. –

Left Munich on 1st May, arriving after nightfall to Klausenburgh. Here I stopped for the night at the Hotel Royale. I had for supper a chicken done up some way with red pepper. The waiter said it was called paprika hendl, and that I should be able to get it anywhere along the Carpathians. I found my smattering of German very useful here.

In the population of Transylvania there are four distinct nationalities: Saxons in the south, and mixed with them the Wallachs, who are the descendants of the Dacians; Magyars in the west, and Szekelys in the east and north. I am going among the latter, who claim to be descended from Attila and the Huns.

I did not sleep well, for I had all sorts of dreams. There was a dog howling all night under my window, which may have had something to do with it.

I had to hurry breakfast, for the train started a little before eight, or rather it ought to have done so, for after rushing to the station at 7.30 I had to sit in the carriage for more than an hour before we began to move. It seems that the further East you go the more unpunctual are the trains. What ought they to be in China?

All day long we seemed to dawdle through a country which was full of beauty of every kind.

Sometimes we saw little towns or castles on the top of steep hills such as we see in old missals; sometimes we ran by rivers and streams which seemed from the wide stony margin on each side of them to be subject to great floods.

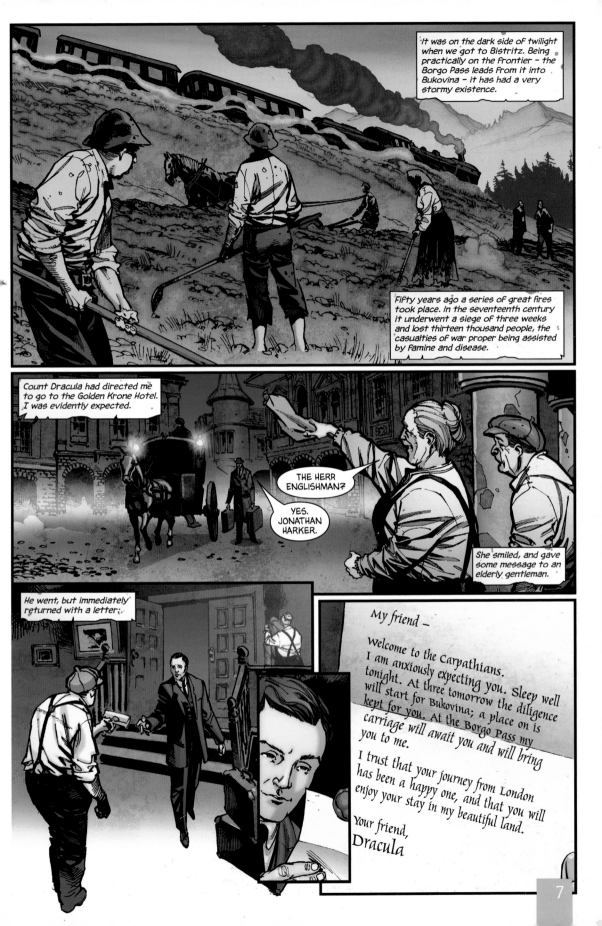

'It was on the dark side of twilight when we got to Bistritz. Being practically on the Frontier – the Borgo Pass leads from it into Bukovina – it has had a very stormy existence.

Fifty years ago a series of great fires took place. In the seventeenth century it underwent a siege of three weeks and lost thirteen thousand people, the casualties of war proper being assisted by famine and disease.

Count Dracula had directed me to go to the Golden Krone Hotel. I was evidently expected.

THE HERR ENGLISHMAN?

YES. JONATHAN HARKER.

She smiled, and gave some message to an elderly gentleman.

He went, but immediately returned with a letter:

My friend –

Welcome to the Carpathians. I am anxiously expecting you. Sleep well tonight. At three tomorrow the diligence will start for Bukovina; a place on is kept for you. At the Borgo Pass my carriage will await you and will bring you to me.

I trust that your journey from London has been a happy one, and that you will enjoy your stay in my beautiful land.

Your friend,
Dracula

I soon lost sight and recollection of ghostly fears in the beauty of the scene as we drove along...

...although had I known the languages which my fellow passengers were speaking, I might not have been able to throw them off so easily.

Beyond the green swelling hills of the Mittel Land rose mighty slopes of forest up to the lofty steeps of the Carpathians themselves. Sometimes the hills were so steep that, despite our driver's haste, the horses could only go slowly.

At last we saw before us the Pass opening out on the eastern side. In the air was the heavy, oppressive sense of thunder.

THERE IS NO **CARRIAGE** HERE. THE HERR IS **NOT** EXPECTED, AFTER ALL.

HE WILL NOW COME ON TO **BUKOVINA**, AND RETURN **TOMORROW** OR THE NEXT DAY.

Whilst he was speaking, the horses began to neigh and snort and plunge wildly. Then, amongst a chorus of screams from the peasants and a universal crossing of themselves, a calèche drove up behind us.

YOU ARE **EARLY** TONIGHT, MY FRIEND.

THE ENGLISH HERR WAS IN A **HURRY**.

THAT IS WHY, I SUPPOSE, YOU WISHED HIM TO GO ON TO **BUKOVINA**.

YOU CANNOT DECEIVE **ME**, MY FRIEND; I KNOW TOO **MUCH**, AND MY HORSES ARE **SWIFT**.

For the **dead** travel **fast**.

With exceeding alacrity my bags were handed out and put in the calèche.

9

We swept into the darkness of the Pass. A dog began to howl somewhere – a long, agonised wailing, as if from fear. The sound was taken up by another dog, and then another and another, till, borne on the wind, a wild howling began which seemed to come from all over the country. Then, far off in the distance, began a louder and sharper howling – that of wolves.

AARRRRWHOOOOOOOOOOOOOOOOOO
AARRRRWHOOOOOOOOOOOOOOOOOO

Suddenly, I saw a faint flickering blue flame.

The driver went rapidly to where the blue flame arose. When he stood between me and the flame he did not obstruct it, for I could see its ghostly figure all the same.

Just then the moon appeared behind the jagged crest of a beetling, pine-clad rock, and by its light I saw a ring of wolves.

As he swept his long arms, as though brushing aside some implacable obstacle, the wolves fell back and back further still.

This was all so strange and uncanny that a dreadful fear came upon me, and I was afraid to speak or move.

Time seemed interminable as we swept on our way. We kept on ascending.

CHAPTER TWO

What sort of place had I come to, and among what kind of people? What sort of grim adventure was it on which I had embarked? Was this a customary incident in the life of a solicitor's clerk sent out to explain the purchase of a London estate to a foreigner?

KER-CLANK

Then there was the sound of rattling chains and the clanking of massive bolts drawn back.

WELCOME TO MY HOUSE! ENTER FREELY AND OF YOUR OWN WILL! COME FREELY. GO SAFELY.

I AM DRACULA. AND I BID YOU WELCOME, MR. HARKER, TO MY HOUSE.

COME IN; THE NIGHT AIR IS CHILL, AND YOU MUST NEED TO EAT AND REST. IT IS LATE, AND MY PEOPLE ARE NOT AVAILABLE.

LET ME SEE TO YOUR COMFORT MYSELF.

5 May. –

I alighted in the courtyard of a vast ruined castle, from whose tall black windows came no ray of light. I must have been asleep, for certainly if I had been fully awake I must have noticed the approach to such a remarkable place.

As I stood, the driver, horses and trap disappeared down one of the dark openings.

I stood in silence where I was, for I did not know what to do. The time I waited seemed endless, and I felt doubts and fears crowding upon me.

YOU WILL NEED, AFTER YOUR JOURNEY, TO REFRESH YOURSELF. I TRUST YOU WILL FIND ALL YOU WISH.

WHEN YOU ARE READY COME INTO THE OTHER ROOM, WHERE YOU WILL FIND YOUR SUPPER PREPARED.

11

I PRAY YOU, BE **SEATED** AND SUP HOW YOU **PLEASE**.

YOU WILL, I TRUST, **EXCUSE** ME THAT I DO NOT JOIN YOU; BUT I HAVE DINED **ALREADY** AND I DO NOT SUP.

I fell to at once on an excellent roast chicken. During the time I was eating it the Count asked me many questions as to my journey, and I told him by degrees all I had experienced.

As the Count leaned over me, I could not repress a shudder. It may have been that his breath was rank, but a horrible feeling of nausea came over me, which, do what I would, I could not conceal.

The Count, evidently noticing it, drew back. We were both silent for a while.

I saw the first dim streak of the coming dawn. There seemed a strange stillness over everything; but as I listened I heard as if from down below in the valley, the howling of many wolves.

LISTEN TO THEM -- THE CHILDREN OF THE **NIGHT**. WHAT **MUSIC** THEY MAKE!

AARRRRRWHOOOOOOOOOOOOOOOOOOOOOO

Ah, SIR, YOU DWELLERS IN THE **CITY** CANNOT ENTER INTO THE FEELINGS OF THE **HUNTER**.

BUT YOU MUST BE **TIRED**. YOUR BEDROOM IS ALL **READY,** AND TOMORROW YOU SHALL SLEEP AS LONG AS YOU **WILL**.

I HAVE TO BE **AWAY** TILL THE AFTERNOON; SO **SLEEP** WELL AND **DREAM** WELL!

12

I am all in a sea of wonders. I doubt; I fear; I think strange things which I dare not confess to my own soul.

GOD **KEEP** ME, IF ONLY FOR THE SAKE OF THOSE **DEAR** TO ME!

7 May. –

I have rested and enjoyed the last twenty-four hours. There are certainly odd deficiencies in the house, considering the extraordinary evidences of wealth which are around me.

The curtains and upholstery are of the costliest and most beautiful fabrics. But still in none of the rooms is there a mirror. I have not seen a servant anywhere, or heard a sound except the howling of wolves.

I looked for something to read. In the library I found, to my great delight, a vast number of English books, whole shelves full of them, and bound volumes of magazines and newspapers – all relating to England and English life and customs and manners.

I HOPE YOU HAD A GOOD NIGHT'S REST. I AM **GLAD** YOU FOUND YOUR WAY IN HERE, FOR I AM SURE THERE IS MUCH THAT WILL **INTEREST** YOU.

THESE HAVE BEEN GOOD **FRIENDS** TO ME. THROUGH THEM I HAVE COME TO **KNOW** YOUR GREAT **ENGLAND**. I **LONG** TO GO THROUGH THE CROWDED STREETS OF YOUR MIGHTY LONDON, TO **SHARE** ITS LIFE, ITS CHANGE, ITS **DEATH**.

BUT **ALAS!** AS YET I ONLY KNOW YOUR TONGUE THROUGH BOOKS.

INDEED, YOU SPEAK EXCELLENTLY.

13

NOT SO. **WELL** I KNOW THAT, DID I MOVE AND SPEAK IN YOUR **LONDON**, NONE THERE ARE WHO WOULD NOT KNOW ME FOR A **STRANGER.** THAT IS **NOT** ENOUGH FOR ME.

HERE I AM NOBLE; AND I AM **MASTER.** I HAVE BEEN SO LONG MASTER THAT I **WOULD** BE MASTER **STILL.**

YOU SHALL REST **HERE** WITH ME A WHILE, SO THAT I MAY LEARN THE ENGLISH **INTONATION,** AND I WOULD THAT YOU **TELL** ME WHEN I MAKE **ERROR.**

I AM WILLING – MIGHT I COME INTO THIS ROOM WHEN I **CHOOSE?**

YOU MAY GO ANYWHERE YOU **WISH** IN THE CASTLE, EXCEPT WHERE THE DOORS ARE **LOCKED,** WHERE OF COURSE YOU WILL NOT **WISH** TO GO.

WE ARE IN **TRANSYLVANIA;** AND TRANSYLVANIA IS **NOT** ENGLAND. OUR WAYS ARE NOT **YOUR** WAYS, AND THERE SHALL BE TO YOU MANY **STRANGE** THINGS.

SUCH AS THE **BLUE FLAME?**

IT IS COMMONLY BELIEVED THAT ON A CERTAIN NIGHT OF THE YEAR, A BLUE FLAME IS SEEN OVER ANY PLACE WHERE **TREASURE** HAS BEEN **CONCEALED.**

BECAUSE YOUR PEASANT IS AT HEART A **COWARD** AND A **FOOL!** THOSE FLAMES ONLY APPEAR ON **ONE** NIGHT. AND ON THAT NIGHT **NO** MAN OF THIS LAND WILL, IF HE CAN HELP IT, STIR **WITHOUT** HIS DOORS.

YOU WOULD NOT, I DARE BE SWORN, BE ABLE TO **FIND** THESE PLACES **AGAIN?**

THERE YOU ARE **RIGHT.** I KNOW NO MORE THAN THE **DEAD** WHERE EVEN TO **LOOK** FOR THEM.

COME, TELL ME OF LONDON AND OF THE **HOUSE** WHICH YOU HAVE PROCURED FOR ME WITH MY OTHER FRIEND **PETER HAWKINS.**

THE ESTATE IS CALLED **CARFAX** --

BUT **HOW** CAN IT HAVE REMAINED SO LONG **UNDISCOVERED** WHEN THERE IS A **SURE** INDEX TO IT?

"IT CONTAINS IN ALL SOME TWENTY ACRES, QUITE SURROUNDED BY A SOLID STONE WALL."

"THERE ARE BUT FEW HOUSES CLOSE AT HAND, ONE BEING A VERY LARGE HOUSE ONLY RECENTLY ADDED TO AND FORMED INTO A PRIVATE **LUNATIC ASYLUM.** IT IS NOT, HOWEVER, VISIBLE FROM THE GROUNDS."

I AM GLAD THAT IT IS **OLD** AND BIG. TO LIVE IN A **NEW** HOUSE WOULD **KILL** ME.

8 May. – I only slept a few hours, and got up. I was just beginning to shave. Suddenly –

GOOD MORNING.

I SEEK **NOT** GAIETY NOR MIRTH. I AM NO LONGER **YOUNG;** AND MY HEART, THROUGH **WEARY** YEARS OF **MOURNING** OVER THE DEAD, IS NOT **ATTUNED** TO MIRTH.

I LOVE THE **SHADE** AND THE **SHADOW,** AND WOULD BE **ALONE** WITH MY THOUGHTS WHEN I MAY.

Somehow his words and his look did not seem to accord.

In starting I had cut myself slightly, for it amazed me that I had not seen him. But there was no reflection of him in the mirror!

HISS!

13

He suddenly made a grab at my throat. I drew away, and his hand touched the string of beads which held the crucifix.

It made an instant change in him, for the fury passed so quickly that I could hardly believe that it was ever there.

TAKE CARE HOW YOU **CUT** YOURSELF. IT IS MORE **DANGEROUS** THAN YOU THINK IN **THIS** COUNTRY.

AND THIS IS THE **WRETCHED** THING THAT HAS DONE THE **MISCHIEF.** IT IS A FOUL BAUBLE OF MAN'S **VANITY.**

AWAY WITH IT!

He flung out the glass, which was shattered on the stones of the courtyard far below. Then he withdrew without a word.

It is very annoying, for I do not see how I am to shave, unless in my watch-case or the bottom of the shaving-pot, which is, fortunately, of metal.

SMASH

I breakfasted alone; I could not find the Count anywhere. After breakfast I did a little exploring in the castle. I found a room looking towards the south. The view was magnificent as the castle is on the very edge of a terrible precipice.

But I am not in heart to describe beauty, for when I had seen the view I explored further; doors, doors, doors everywhere, and all locked and bolted.

THE CASTLE IS A VERITABLE **PRISON,** AND I AM A PRISONER!

CHAPTER THREE

Midnight. –

IS IT A WONDER THAT WE **SZEKELYS** WERE A **CONQUERING** RACE; THAT WE ARE **PROUD?** TO US FOR **CENTURIES** WAS TRUSTED THE **GUARDING** OF THE FRONTIER OF TURKEY-LAND.

WHO WAS IT BUT ONE OF MY **OWN** RACE WHO AS **VIOVODE** CROSSED THE DANUBE AND **BEAT** THE TURK ON HIS **OWN** GROUND?

THIS WAS A **DRACULA** INDEED. THE WARLIKE DAYS ARE **OVER**. BLOOD IS TOO **PRECIOUS** A THING IN THESE DAYS OF DISHONOURABLE **PEACE**.

12 May. –
He began by asking me questions on legal matters... about solicitors... and about shipping goods to English ports...

I COULD BE AT LIBERTY TO DIRECT **MYSELF?**

SUCH IS OFTEN DONE BY MEN OF BUSINESS.

GOOD!

THEN WRITE **NOW**, MY YOUNG FRIEND, TO OUR FRIEND MR. PETER HAWKINS AND TO ANY OTHER; AND SAY, IF IT WILL **PLEASE** YOU, THAT YOU SHALL **STAY** WITH ME UNTIL A **MONTH** FROM NOW.

My heart grew cold at the thought.

DO YOU WISH ME TO STAY SO **LONG?**

I DESIRE IT **MUCH**; NAY, I WILL TAKE **NO** REFUSAL. IT WAS UNDERSTOOD THAT **MY** NEEDS **ONLY** WERE TO BE CONSULTED.

I **PRAY** YOU, MY **GOOD** YOUNG **FRIEND**, THAT YOU WILL **NOT** DISCOURSE OF THINGS **OTHER** THAN **BUSINESS** IN YOUR LETTERS.

IT WILL DOUBTLESS **PLEASE** YOUR FRIENDS TO KNOW THAT YOU ARE **WELL**, AND THAT YOU LOOK FORWARD TO GETTING **HOME** TO THEM.

IS IT NOT **SO?**

LET ME **WARN** YOU THAT SHOULD YOU **LEAVE** THESE ROOMS YOU WILL NOT BY ANY CHANCE GO TO **SLEEP** IN ANY **OTHER** PART OF THE CASTLE.

IT IS **OLD**, AND HAS MANY **MEMORIES**, AND THERE ARE **BAD DREAMS** FOR THOSE WHO SLEEP **UNWISELY**.

BE WARNED! IN YOUR **OWN** CHAMBER, YOUR **REST** WILL BE **SAFE**.

I shall not fear to sleep in any place where he is not. I have placed the crucifix over my bed – I imagine that my rest is thus freer from dreams; and there it shall remain.

I must have fallen asleep; I hope so, but I fear, for all that followed was startlingly real. I was not alone. I felt in my heart a wicked, burning desire that they would kiss me with those red lips.

GO ON! YOU ARE THE FIRST, AND WE SHALL FOLLOW; YOURS IS THE RIGHT TO BEGIN.

HE IS YOUNG AND STRONG; THERE ARE KISSES FOR US ALL.

I closed my eyes in a languorous ecstasy and waited – waited with beating heart.

But at that instant another sensation swept through me. I was conscious of the presence of the Count.

HOW DARE YOU TOUCH HIM, ANY OF YOU?

HOW DARE YOU CAST EYES ON HIM WHEN I HAD FORBIDDEN IT?

BACK, I TELL YOU ALL! THIS MAN BELONGS TO ME!

BEWARE HOW YOU MEDDLE WITH HIM, OR YOU'LL HAVE TO DEAL WITH ME.

YOU YOURSELF NEVER LOVED; YOU NEVER LOVE!

31 May.

When I woke, every scrap of paper was gone, and with it all my notes and memoranda.

17 June.

Two great leiter-wagons, driven by Slovaks, delivered great square boxes that were evidently empty.

24 June, before morning. – I heard a sound in the courtyard without – the agonised cry of a woman.

Somewhere high overhead, I heard the voice of the Count calling. His call seemed to be answered from far and wide by the howling of wolves.

GRRRAAAH

MONSTER, GIVE ME MY CHILD!

There was no cry from the woman and the howling of the wolves was short.

I could not pity her, for I knew now what had become of her child, and she was better dead.

GRRRR

How can I escape from this dreadful thrall of night and gloom and fear?

25 June, morning.

LET ME NOT THINK OF IT. ACTION! IF I COULD ONLY GET INTO HIS ROOM!

BUT THERE IS NO POSSIBLE WAY. THE DOOR IS ALWAYS LOCKED.

I HAVE SEEN HIM CRAWL FROM HIS WINDOW; WHY SHOULD I NOT IMITATE HIM. THE CHANCES ARE DESPERATE, BUT MY NEED IS MORE DESPERATE STILL.

22

I ventured out on the desperate way...

...to the Count's window.

The room was empty! I looked for the key, but could not find it anywhere.

I MUST MAKE FURTHER EXAMINATION.

There was a great heap of gold of all kinds, covered with a film of dust, as though it had lain long in the ground.

A heavy door led through a stone passage to a circular stairway, which went steeply down.

I descended.

At the bottom came a deathly, sickly odour of old earth newly turned. I found myself in an old, ruined chapel, which had evidently been used as a graveyard.

The ground had recently been dug over, and the earth placed in the great wooden boxes, manifestly those which had been brought by the Slovaks.

23

I went down even into the vaults.

There, in one of the great boxes, lay the Count! He was either dead or asleep, I could not say which – for the eyes were open and stony but without the glassiness of death.

I fled from the place and, regaining my own chamber, tried to think...

29 June. –
Today is the date of my last letter. Again I saw him leave the castle by the same window, and in my clothes. I dared not wait to see him return, for I feared to see those weird sisters. I came back to the library, and read there till I fell asleep.

I was awakened by the Count.

TOMORROW, MY FRIEND, WE MUST **PART.** YOU RETURN TO YOUR BEAUTIFUL **ENGLAND,** I TO SOME WORK WHICH MAY HAVE SUCH AN END THAT WE MAY **NEVER** MEET.

YOUR LETTER **HOME** HAS BEEN DESPATCHED; TOMORROW I SHALL NOT BE HERE, BUT ALL SHALL BE **READY** FOR YOUR **JOURNEY.**

WHY MAY I NOT GO **TONIGHT?**

BECAUSE MY COACHMAN AND HORSES ARE AWAY ON A MISSION.

I WOULD **WALK** WITH PLEASURE. I WANT TO GET AWAY AT **ONCE.**

He opened the door.

YOU ENGLISH HAVE A SAYING, "WELCOME THE COMING, SPEED THE PARTING GUEST."

HAOOOHH

NOT AN **HOUR** SHALL YOU WAIT IN MY HOUSE **AGAINST** YOUR WILL.

COME!

The howling of the wolves without grew louder and angrier. I was to be given to the wolves, and at my own instigation.

24

SHUT THE DOOR; I SHALL WAIT TILL MORNING!

The Count threw the door shut.

Outside the door, I heard the voice of the Count...

BACK, **BACK,** TO YOUR **OWN** PLACE! YOUR TIME IS NOT **YET** COME.

WAIT. HAVE PATIENCE. TOMORROW NIGHT IS YOURS!

HA HA HA HA HA

30 June, morning. – The door down the hall was locked. A wild desire took me to obtain that key at any risk.

Without a pause I scrambled down the wall, as before. I knew now well enough where to find the monster I sought.

I knew I must search the body for the key; and then I saw something which filled my very soul with horror.

The Count looked as if his youth had been half renewed. He lay like a filthy leech, exhausted with his repletion.

This was the being I was helping to transfer to London, where he might create a new and ever-widening circle of semi-demons to batten on the helpless.
The very thought drove me mad. A terrible desire came upon me to rid the world of such a monster.

The eyes fell full upon me, with all their blaze of basilisk horror. The sight seemed to paralyse me.

The shovel turned and merely made a deep gash above the forehead. It fell from my hand.

PANK

The last glimpse I had was of the bloated face, blood-stained and fixed with a grin of malice which would have held its own in the nethermost hell.

I thought and thought what should be my next move, but my brain seemed to be on fire. I heard the rolling of heavy wheels and the cracking of whips; the Szgany and the Slovaks of whom the Count had spoken were coming. I ran from the place...

...and gained the Count's room. I heard a sound of many tramping feet and the crash of weights being set down heavily, doubtless the boxes, with their freight of earth. There was a sound of hammering; it was the box being nailed down. Then, in the courtyard the rolling of heavy wheels, the cracking of whips, and the chorus of the Szgany as they passed into the distance.

CHAPTER FIVE

Letter from Miss Mina Murray to Miss Lucy Westenra:

9 May.

My dearest Lucy, -

Forgive my long delay in writing, but I have been simply overwhelmed by work. The life of an assistant schoolmistress is sometimes trying.

I am longing to be with you, and by the sea, where we can talk together freely and build our castles in the air. I have been working very hard lately, because I want to keep up with Jonathan's studies, and I have been practicing shorthand very assiduously. When we are married I shall be able to be useful to Jonathan, and if I can stenograph well enough I can take down what he wants to say in this way and write it out for him on the typewriter.

I have just had a few hurried lines from Jonathan from Transylvania. He is well, and will be returning in about a week. I am longing to hear all his news. It must be so nice to see strange countries. I wonder if Jonathan and I shall ever see them together.

Your loving

Mina.

Tell me all the news when you write. I hear rumours of a tall, handsome man???

Letter, Lucy Westenra
to Mina Murray:

My dearest Mina, –

Someone has evidently been telling
tales. The tall man is Mr. Holmwood.
He often comes to see us, and he
and mamma get on very well
together; they have so many things
to talk about in common. We met
some time ago a man that would
just do for you, if you were not
already engaged to Jonathan.
He is a doctor and really clever.
Just fancy! He has an immense
lunatic asylum all under his own
care. Mr. Holmwood introduced me
to him, and he called here to see us,
and often comes now. I think he is
one of the most resolute men
I ever saw, and yet the most calm.
He seems absolutely imperturbable.
His name is Dr. John Seward.

Mina, we have told all our secrets to
each other since we were children.
Oh, Mina, couldn't you guess?
I love Arthur Holmwood.
I am blushing as I write, for
although I think he loves me,
he has not told me so in words.
But, oh, Mina, I love him; I love him;
<u>I love him!</u>

Good-night.

Lucy.
P.S. – I need not tell you this is a
secret.

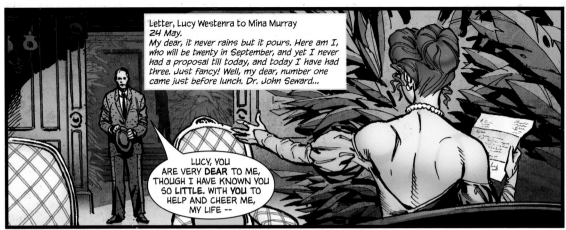

Letter, Lucy Westenra to Mina Murray
24 May.
My dear, it never rains but it pours. Here am I, who will be twenty in September, and yet I never had a proposal till today, and today I have had three. Just fancy! Well, my dear, number one came just before lunch. Dr. John Seward...

LUCY, YOU ARE VERY **DEAR** TO ME, THOUGH I HAVE KNOWN YOU SO **LITTLE.** WITH **YOU** TO HELP AND CHEER ME, MY LIFE --

He was going to tell me how unhappy he would be if I did not care for him, but when he saw me cry...

-- I AM A **BRUTE.** I WILL NOT ADD TO YOUR PRESENT TROUBLE.

DO YOU... CARE ALREADY FOR ANYONE **ELSE?**

I DO NOT WANT TO WRING YOUR **CONFIDENCE** FROM YOU, BUT ONLY TO KNOW, BECAUSE IF A WOMAN'S **HEART** IS FREE A MAN MIGHT HAVE **HOPE.**

THERE **IS** SOMEONE.

I HOPE YOU WILL BE **HAPPY.** IF YOU EVER WANT A **FRIEND** YOU MUST COUNT **ME** ONE OF YOUR **BEST.**

Being proposed to is all very nice, but it isn't at all a happy thing when you see a poor fellow going away broken-hearted.

Well, my dear, number two came after lunch. He is such a nice fellow, an American from Texas, and he looks so young and so fresh that it seems almost impossible that he has been to so many places and has had such adventures.
Mr. Quincey P. Morris found me alone...

MISS LUCY, I **KNOW** I AIN'T GOOD ENOUGH TO REGULATE THE **FIXIN'S** OF YOUR LITTLE **SHOES,** BUT WON'T YOU JUST HITCH UP **ALONGSIDE** OF ME AND LET US GO DOWN THE LONG ROAD **TOGETHER** DRIVING IN **DOUBLE HARNESS?**

I DO NOT KNOW **ANYTHING** OF HITCHING AND I AM NOT BROKEN TO **HARNESS** AT ALL YET.

30

LUCY, YOU ARE AN **HONEST-HEARTED** GIRL. TELL ME, LIKE ONE GOOD FELLOW TO ANOTHER, IS THERE ANYONE **ELSE** THAT YOU CARE FOR?

AND IF THERE **IS**, I'LL NEVER TROUBLE YOU A HAIR'S BREADTH **AGAIN**, BUT WILL BE, IF YOU WILL **LET ME**, A VERY FAITHFUL **FRIEND**.

I burst into tears.

I am glad to say that, though I was crying, I was able to look into Mr. Morris's brave eyes, and I told him out straight:

YES, THERE IS SOMEONE I LOVE, THOUGH **HE** HAS NOT TOLD ME YET THAT HE EVEN **LOVES** ME.

DON'T CRY, MY DEAR.

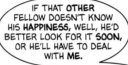

IF THAT **OTHER** FELLOW DOESN'T KNOW HIS **HAPPINESS**, WELL, HE'D BETTER LOOK FOR IT **SOON**, OR HE'LL HAVE TO DEAL WITH **ME**.

LITTLE GIRL, YOUR **HONESTY** AND **PLUCK** HAVE MADE ME A **FRIEND**, AND THAT'S **RARER** THAN A LOVER; IT'S MORE **UNSELFISH** ANYHOW.

THANK YOU FOR YOUR SWEET **HONESTY** TO ME, AND **GOOD-BYE**.

OH, WHY MUST A MAN LIKE THAT BE MADE **UNHAPPY** WHEN THERE ARE **LOTS** OF GIRLS ABOUT WHO WOULD **WORSHIP** THE VERY GROUND HE **TROD** ON?

I KNOW I WOULD IF I WERE **FREE**, ONLY I DON'T **WANT** TO BE FREE.

I needn't tell you of number three, need I? Besides, it was all so confused; it seemed only a moment from his coming into the room till both his arms were round me, and he was kissing me.

I am very, very happy, and I don't know what I have done to deserve it. I must only try in the future to show that I am not ungrateful for all God's goodness to me in sending to me such a lover, such a husband, and such a friend.

Dr. Seward's Diary
(kept in phonograph)

25 April. – Cannot eat,
cannot rest, so diary
instead. Since my rebuff
of yesterday I have a
sort of empty feeling;
nothing in the world
seems of sufficient
importance to be
worth the doing.

AS I KNEW THAT THE ONLY CURE WAS **WORK,** I WENT DOWN AMONGST THE **PATIENTS.**

I PICKED OUT ONE WHO HAS AFFORDED ME A STUDY OF **MUCH** INTEREST. HE IS SO **UNLIKE** THE NORMAL LUNATIC THAT I HAVE DETERMINED TO **UNDERSTAND** HIM AS WELL AS I CAN.

TODAY I SEEMED TO GET **NEARER** THAN EVER BEFORE TO THE **HEART** OF HIS **MYSTERY.**

R M Renfield –

Sanguine temperament;
great physical strength;
morbidly excitable;
periods of gloom ending
in some fixed idea which
I cannot make out.

His redeeming quality
is a love of animals,
though his pets are of
odd sorts. Just now his
hobby is catching flies.

5 June. –
Renfield has selfishness,
secrecy and purpose. I wish
I could get at what is the
object of the latter.

18 June. –
He has turned his
mind now to SPIDERS.

He keeps feeding them with
his flies, although he has
used half his food in
attracting more flies from
outside to his room.

CHAPTER SIX

Mina Murray's Journal

24 July. Whitby. –

Lucy met me at the station, and
we drove up to the house at the
Crescent in which they have rooms.
This is a lovely place. There are
walks, with seats beside them,
through the churchyard; and
people go and sit there all day
long looking at the beautiful view.

They have a legend here that
when a ship is lost bells are
heard out at sea. I must ask the
old man about this. He is a funny
old man. He must be awfully old.

1 August. –

Mr. Swales tells me that he is
nearly a hundred, and that he was
a sailor in the fishing fleet when
Waterloo was fought. He is, I am
afraid, a very sceptical person.

IT BE ALL **FOOL-TALK,** AN' NOWT
ELSE. THESE BANS AN' WAFTS AN'
BOH-GHOSTS AN' BAR-GUESTS AN'
BOGLES AN' ALL ANENT THEM
IS ONLY FIT TO SET BAIRNS
AN' DIZZY WOMEN
A-BELDERIN'.

THEY
BE **NOWT**
BUT **AIR-BLEBS!**
IT MAKES ME
IREFUL TO THINK
O' THEM.

One by one they left. Lucy and I sat
a while, and she told me again about
Arthur and their coming marriage.
That made me just a little heart-sick,
for I haven't heard from Jonathan for
a whole month. I hope there cannot
be anything the matter with him.

I wonder where Jonathan
is and if he is thinking of
me! I wish he were here.

Dr. Seward's Diary
1 July. –
Renfield's spiders are now becoming as great a nuisance as his flies, and today I told him that he must get rid of them.

BUZZZZZ

He looked very sad at this.

He disgusted me much while with him, for when a horrid blow-fly, bloated with some carrion food, buzzed into the room, he caught it, put it in his mouth and ATE it.

I scolded him for it, but he argued...

IT IS VERY GOOD AND VERY **WHOLESOME**. IT IS **LIFE, STRONG LIFE**, AND GIVES LIFE TO **ME**.

This gave me an idea. I must watch how he gets rid of his spiders.

8 July. –
There is a METHOD in his MADNESS and the rudimentary idea in my mind is growing. Things remain as they were except that he has parted with some of his pets and got a new one. He has managed to get a SPARROW, and has already partially tamed it.

19 July. –
My friend has now a whole colony of sparrows, and his flies and spiders are almost obliterated.

I WANT TO ASK YOU A VERY, VERY GREAT **FAVOUR**, DOCTOR SEWARD.

WHAT IS IT?

34

A *KITTEN*, A NICE LITTLE, SLEEK, PLAYFUL KITTEN, THAT I CAN *PLAY* WITH, AND *TEACH*, AND FEED – AND *FEED* – AND *FEED*!

I FEAR IT WILL NOT BE *POSSIBLE* AT PRESENT, BUT I WILL SEE ABOUT IT.

His face fell...

... and I could see a warning of danger in it. For there was a sudden fierce, sidelong look which meant KILLING. The man is an undeveloped homicidal maniac.

I shall test him with his present craving and see how it will work out; then I shall know more.

20 July. –
Visited Renfield very early. There were a few feathers about the room, and on his pillow a drop of blood.

WHERE ARE THE BIRDS, RENFIELD?

THEY HAVE ALL FLOWN *AWAY*.

MY BELIEF IS, DOCTOR, THAT HE HAS *EATEN* HIS BIRDS, AND THAT HE JUST *TOOK* AND ATE THEM RAW!

I gave Renfield a strong opiate tonight, enough to make even him sleep. I shall call him a ZOOPHAGOUS (life-eating) maniac; what he desires is to absorb as many lives as he can, and he has laid himself out to achieve it in a cumulative way.

He gave many flies to one spider and many spiders to one bird, and then wanted a cat to eat the many birds. What would have been his later steps?

I wonder at how many lives he values a MAN, or if at only one.

OH, LUCY, LUCY, I CANNOT BE *ANGRY* WITH YOU, NOR CAN I BE ANGRY WITH MY *FRIEND* WHOSE HAPPINESS IS *YOURS*; BUT I MUST ONLY WAIT ON HOPELESS AND WORK. *WORK!* WORK!

IF I ONLY COULD HAVE AS *STRONG* A *CAUSE* AS MY POOR MAD FRIEND THERE TO MAKE ME WORK, THAT WOULD BE INDEED HAPPINESS.

35

Mina Murray's Journal   26 July. –

I had not heard from Jonathan for some time, and was very concerned; but yesterday dear Mr. Hawkins sent me a letter from him. It says that he is just starting for home from Castle Dracula. That is not like Jonathan; I do not understand it, and it makes me uneasy.

Lucy, although she is so well, has lately taken to her old habit of walking in her sleep. Her mother has spoken to me about it, and we have decided that I am to lock the door of our room every night.

Lucy is to be married in the autumn, and she is already planning out her dresses. Hon. Arthur Holmwood, the only son of Lord Godalming, is coming up here as soon as he can leave town, for his father is not very well. I think dear Lucy is counting the moments till he comes.

6 August. –

Still no news.
The horizon is lost in a grey mist. The clouds are piled up like giant rocks, and there is a "brool" over the sea that sounds like some presage of doom. Dark figures are shrouded in the mist, and seem "men like trees walking".

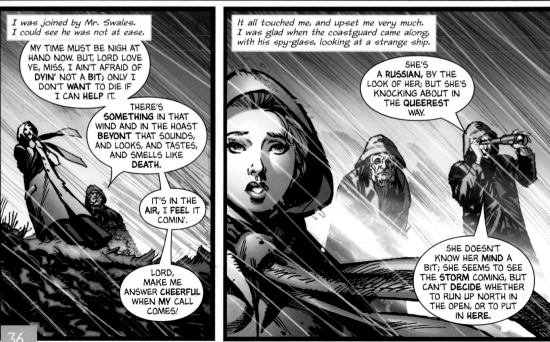

I was joined by Mr. Swales. I could see he was not at ease.

MY TIME MUST BE NIGH AT HAND NOW. BUT, LORD LOVE YE, MISS, I AIN'T AFRAID OF **DYIN'** NOT A BIT; ONLY I DON'T **WANT** TO DIE IF I CAN HELP IT.

THERE'S **SOMETHING** IN THAT WIND AND IN THE HOAST **BEYONT** THAT SOUNDS, AND LOOKS, AND TASTES, AND SMELLS LIKE **DEATH**.

IT'S IN THE AIR, I FEEL IT COMIN'.

LORD, MAKE ME ANSWER **CHEERFUL** WHEN **MY** CALL COMES!

It all touched me, and upset me very much. I was glad when the coastguard came along, with his spy-glass, looking at a strange ship.

SHE'S A **RUSSIAN**, BY THE LOOK OF HER; BUT SHE'S KNOCKING ABOUT IN THE **QUEEREST** WAY.

SHE DOESN'T KNOW HER **MIND** A BIT; SHE SEEMS TO SEE THE **STORM** COMING, BUT CAN'T **DECIDE** WHETHER TO RUN UP NORTH IN THE OPEN, OR TO PUT IN **HERE**.

CHAPTER SEVEN

CUTTING FROM THE DAILYGRAPH, 8 AUGUST:

One of the greatest and suddenest storms on record has just been experienced here, with results both strange and unique. A little after midnight came a strange sound from over the sea; then without warning the tempest broke. The waves rose in growing fury. The wind, leaping from wave to wave as it rushed at headlong speed, swept the strange schooner before the blast, and gained the safety of the harbour.

The searchlight followed her, and a shudder ran through all who saw her, for lashed to the helm was a corpse. No other form could be seen on deck at all.

The ship had found the harbour, unsteered save by the hand of a dead man! The coastguard said the man must have tied up his own hands, fastening the knots with his teeth.

9 August. –

The schooner is a Russian from Varna, and is called the *Demeter,* with only a small amount of cargo – a number of great wooden boxes filled with mould. This cargo was consigned to a Whitby solicitor, Mr. S. F. Billington, who took possession of the goods. The Russian consul took formal possession of the ship.

A good deal of interest was abroad concerning the dog which landed when the ship struck. It seems to have disappeared from the town.

Early this morning a large dog, a mastiff belonging to a coal merchant, was found dead. It had been fighting, for its throat was torn away, and its belly was slit open as if with a savage claw.

Log of The Demeter

(Varna to Whitby)

On 6 July set sail. Crew, five hands...

On 13 July crew dissatisfied about something.

On 14 July, anxious about crew. They only told mate there was something, and crossed themselves.

On 16 July, mate reported Petrofsky missing.

17 July. -- Olgaren confided that he thought there was a strange man aboard the ship. We left no corner unsearched. Found no one. Men much relieved.

24 July. -- There seems some doom over this ship. Last night another man lost. -- disappeared.

28 July. -- Four days in hell, knocking about in a sort of maelstrom. No sleep for anyone.

29 July. -- Another tragedy. Night watchman lost.

30 July. -- Both men of watch and steersman missing. Only self and mate and one hand left to work ship.

1 August. -- Two days of fog. We seem to be drifting to some terrible doom.

2 August. -- One more gone. Only God can guide us in the fog; and God seems to have deserted us.

3 August. Midnight.

MATE!

IT IS HERE! I KNOW IT, NOW. ON THE WATCH LAST NIGHT I SAW IT, LIKE A MAN, TALL AND THIN, AND GHASTLY PALE.

IT WAS IN THE BOWS, AND LOOKING OUT.

I CREPT BEHIND IT, AND GAVE IT MY KNIFE, BUT THE KNIFE WENT THROUGH IT, EMPTY AS THE AIR.

BUT IT IS HERE, AND I'LL FIND IT. IT IS IN THE HOLD, PERHAPS, IN ONE OF THOSE BOXES. I'LL UNSCREW THEM ONE BY ONE AND SEE. YOU WORK THE HELM.

I could not leave the helm. He is stark, raving mad and it's no use my trying to stop him.

SAVE ME!

SAVE ME!

HE IS THERE! I KNOW THE SECRET NOW!

THE SEA WILL SAVE ME FROM HIM, AND IT IS ALL THAT IS LEFT!

4 August. -- The mate was right to jump overboard. It is better to die like a man. But I am captain, and I must not leave my ship. If we are wrecked, mayhap this log may be found and those who find it may understand. God and the Blessed Virgin and the Saints help a poor ignorant soul trying to do his duty...

39

Mina Murray's Journal 10 August. -

The funeral of the poor sea-captain today was most touching. Poor Lucy seemed much upset. She was restless and uneasy, and I think that her dreaming at night is telling on her. She does not understand it herself.

There is an additional cause in that poor old Mr. Swales was found dead this morning on our seat, his neck being broken. He had evidently, as the doctor said, fallen back in the seat with some form of fright, for there was a look of fear and horror on his face that the men said made them shudder. Poor dear old man! Perhaps he had seen Death with his dying eyes!

11 August, 3am. -

CHAPTER EIGHT

We have had such an adventure, such an agonizing experience. Suddenly I became broad awake with a horrible sense of fear upon me. Lucy's bed was empty.

The door was shut, but not locked, as I had left it.

I looked in all the rooms in the house. Finally, I came to the hall-door and found it open. There was no time to think of what might happen; I took a big, heavy shawl...

...and ran out along the North Terrace.

At the edge of the West Cliff I looked across the harbour to the East Cliff, in the hope or fear - I don't know which - of seeing Lucy in our favourite seat.

The silver light of the moon struck a half-reclining figure, snowy white. It seemed to me as though something dark stood behind the seat, and bent over it. What it was, whether man or beast, I could not tell.

LUCY! LUCY!

Something raised a head.

Lucy did not answer.

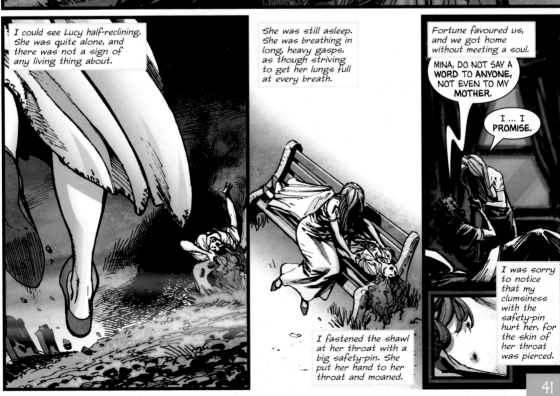

I could see Lucy half-reclining. She was quite alone, and there was not a sign of any living thing about.

She was still asleep. She was breathing in long, heavy gasps, as though striving to get her lungs full at every breath.

Fortune favoured us, and we got home without meeting a soul.

MINA, DO NOT SAY A WORD TO ANYONE, NOT EVEN TO MY MOTHER.

I ... I PROMISE.

I fastened the shawl at her throat with a big safety-pin. She put her hand to her throat and moaned.

I was sorry to notice that my clumsiness with the safety-pin hurt her, for the skin of her throat was pierced.

41

Letter, Samuel F. Billington & Son, Solicitors, Whitby,
to Messrs. Carter Paterson & Co., London

17 August

Dear Sirs, -

Herewith please receive invoice of goods sent by Great
Northern Railway. Same are to be delivered to Carfax near
Purfleet, immediately on receipt at goods station King's Cross.
The house is at present empty, but enclosed please find keys, all
of which are labelled.

You will please deposit the boxes, fifty in number, which form
the consignment, in the partially ruined building forming
part of the house. Your agent will easily recognise the locality,
as it is the ancient chapel of the mansion.

The goods will be due at King's Cross at 4:30 tomorrow
afternoon. As our client wishes the delivery to be made as soon
as possible, we shall be obliged by your having teams ready at
King's Cross at the time named and forthwith conveying the
goods to destination.

You are to leave the keys on coming away in the main hall of
the house, where the proprietor may get them on his entering
the house by means of his duplicate key.

Faithfully yours,

Samuel F. Billington & Son

42

HIS RED EYES **AGAIN!** THEY ARE JUST THE **SAME!**

15 August. –
Rose later than usual. Lucy was tired, and slept on. Arthur's father is better, and wants the marriage to come off soon. Lucy is full of joy, and her mother is glad and sorry at once...

I AM GRIEVED TO **LOSE** LUCY AS MY VERY OWN, BUT I AM REJOICED THAT LUCY WILL SOON HAVE SOMEONE TO **PROTECT** HER. YOU MUST KEEP THIS **SECRET** – I HAVE NOT TOLD LUCY – BUT MY **DOCTOR** HAS TOLD ME THAT WITHIN A FEW MONTHS I MUST **DIE,** FOR MY **HEART** IS **WEAKENING.**

A SUDDEN **SHOCK** WOULD BE ALMOST SURE TO KILL ME.

We were wise to keep from her the affair of the dreadful night of Lucy's sleep-walking.

17 August. –
No news from Jonathan, and Lucy seems to be growing weaker, whilst her mother's hours are numbering to a close.

THE TINY WOUNDS ON HER THROAT SEEM ***NOT*** *TO HAVE* ***HEALED.*** *IF ANYTHING, THEY ARE* ***LARGER*** *THAN BEFORE.*

UNLESS THEY HEAL WITHIN A **DAY** OR **TWO,** I SHALL INSIST ON THE **DOCTOR** SEEING ABOUT THEM.

19 August.
Lucy is ever so much better.
Last night she slept well all night, and did not disturb me once.

JOY! AT LAST, **NEWS** OF **JONATHAN.** THE DEAR FELLOW HAS BEEN ILL.

I AM TO LEAVE IN THE **MORNING** AND TO GO OVER TO JONATHAN AND TO HELP TO **NURSE** HIM IF NECESSARY, AND TO BRING HIM **HOME.**

Letter, Sister Agatha, Hospital of St. Joseph and Ste. Mary, Buda-Pesth, To Miss Wilhelmina Murray

Dear Madam, -

I write by desire of Mr. Jonathan Harker, who is himself not strong enough to write, though progressing well, thanks to God and St. Joseph and Ste. Mary. He has been under our care for six weeks, suffering from a violent brain fever.

He wishes me to convey his love. He will require some few weeks' rest in our sanatorium, but will then return.

In his delirium, his ravings have been dreadful; of wolves and poison and blood; of ghosts and demons; and I fear to say of what. Be assured that he is well cared for. He has won all hearts by his sweetness and gentleness. There are, I pray, many, many happy years for you both.

Sister Agatha

Dr. Seward's Diary
19 August. -
Strange and sudden change in Renfield last night. He would not condescend to talk with the attendant.

WHERE ARE YOUR PETS?

I DON'T CARE A PIN ABOUT THEM. THE MASTER IS AT HAND.

YOU DON'T MEAN TO TELL ME THAT YOU DON'T CARE ABOUT SPIDERS?

THE BRIDE-MAIDENS REJOICE THE EYES THAT WAIT THE COMING OF THE BRIDE; BUT WHEN THE BRIDE DRAWETH NIGH, THEN THE MAIDENS SHINE NOT TO THE EYES THAT ARE FILLED.

He would not explain himself.

Later.-- I had lain tossing about, and had heard the clock strike only twice, when the night-watchman came to me, to say that Renfield had ESCAPED.

I threw on my clothes and ran down at once.

As I got through the belt of trees I saw a white figure scale the high wall which separates our grounds from those of the deserted house.

GET THREE OR FOUR MEN **IMMEDIATELY** AND FOLLOW ME INTO THE GROUNDS OF **CARFAX!**

OUR FRIEND MAY BE **DANGEROUS!**

I found him pressed close against the old iron-bound oak door of the chapel.

I AM **HERE** TO DO YOUR BIDDING, MASTER. I AM YOUR **SLAVE**, AND YOU WILL REWARD ME, FOR I SHALL BE **FAITHFUL.**

I HAVE **WORSHIPPED** YOU LONG AND AFAR OFF.

NOW THAT YOU ARE **NEAR** I AWAIT YOUR **COMMANDS**, AND YOU WILL NOT PASS ME BY, WILL YOU, DEAR MASTER, IN YOUR DISTRIBUTION OF **GOOD** THINGS??

He was more like a wild BEAST than a man.

I never saw a lunatic in such a paroxysm of rage before; and I hope I shall not again.

ALGGHGH

I SHALL BE **PATIENT,** MASTER. IT IS COMING – COMING – **COMING!**

He is safe now at any rate. His cries are awful, but the silences are more deadly, for he means MURDER in every turn and movement.

45

CHAPTER NINE

Letter, Mina Harker to Lucy Westenra

Buda-Pesth, 24 August.

My Dearest Lucy, –

I found my dear one, oh, so thin and pale and weak-looking. He is only a wreck of himself, and he does not remember anything that has happened to him for a long time past.

He has had some terrible shock and I fear it might tax his poor brain if he were to try to recall it.

WILHELMINA – YOU KNOW, DEAR, MY IDEAS OF THE **TRUST** BETWEEN HUSBAND AND WIFE: THERE SHOULD BE NO **SECRET**, NO **CONCEALMENT**.

I HAVE HAD A GREAT **SHOCK**, AND I DO NOT KNOW IF IT WAS ALL REAL OR THE DREAMING OF A **MADMAN**. THE SECRET IS **HERE**, AND I DO NOT **WANT** TO **KNOW** IT.

I WANT TO TAKE UP MY LIFE HERE, WITH OUR **MARRIAGE**. ARE YOU WILLING TO SHARE MY **IGNORANCE**?

HERE IS THE **BOOK**. TAKE IT AND KEEP IT, **READ** IT IF YOU WILL, BUT NEVER LET **ME** KNOW; UNLESS SOME SOLEMN DUTY SHOULD COME UPON ME TO GO **BACK** TO THE BITTER HOURS, ASLEEP OR AWAKE, SANE OR MAD, RECORDED **HERE**.

He was exhausted, and I put the book under his pillow. I have asked Sister Agatha to let our wedding be this afternoon.

THAT AFTERNOON...

I WILL.

I AM THE **HAPPIEST** WOMAN IN ALL THE WIDE WORLD.

I HAVE NOTHING TO GIVE YOU EXCEPT **MYSELF**, MY LIFE, AND MY **TRUST**, AND WITH THESE GO MY LOVE AND DUTY FOR **ALL** THE DAYS OF MY LIFE.

When he kissed me, it was a solemn pledge between us...

Letter, Lucy Westenra to Mina Harker

Whitby, 30 August.

My dearest Mina, -

Oceans of love and millions of kisses, and may you soon be in your own home with your husband. This strong air would soon restore Jonathan; it has quite restored me. I am full of life, and sleep well.

Arthur is here. We are to be married on 28 September. Mother sends her love. She seems better, poor dear.

Lucy

Dr. Seward's Diary

23 August. – Another night adventure. Again he went into the grounds of the deserted house.

ARGH!

When he saw me he became FURIOUS, and had not the attendants seized him in time, he would have tried to KILL me.

He suddenly redoubled his efforts...

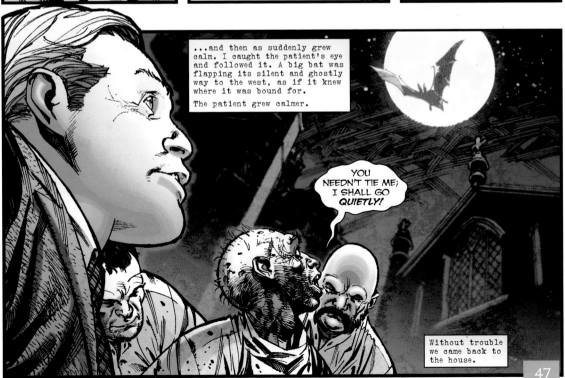

...and then as suddenly grew calm. I caught the patient's eye and followed it. A big bat was flapping its silent and ghostly way to the west, as if it knew where it was bound for.

The patient grew calmer.

YOU NEEDN'T TIE ME; I SHALL GO QUIETLY!

Without trouble we came back to the house.

47

Lucy Westenra's Diary

25 August. —

More bad dreams. I wish I could remember them. This morning I am horribly weak. My face is ghastly pale, and my throat pains me. It must be something wrong with my lungs, for I don't seem ever to get air enough.

Letter, Arthur Holmwood To Dr. Seward

31 August.

My dear Jack, —

I want you to do me a favour. Lucy is ill, and is getting worse every day. I ask if you would see her. It will be a painful task for you, I know, old friend, but it is for her sake, and I must not hesitate to ask, or you to act. I am filled with anxiety, and I want to consult with you alone after you have seen her. Do not fail!

ARTHUR

Letter From Dr. Seward To Arthur Holmwood.

With regard to Miss Westenra's health, I hasten to let you know that in my opinion there is not any malady that I know of. She said to me very sweetly:

I CANNOT TELL YOU HOW I **LOATHE** TALKING ABOUT **MYSELF.**

A DOCTOR'S CONFIDENCE IS **SACRED**, BUT ARTHUR IS **GRIEVOUSLY** ANXIOUS ABOUT YOU.

TELL ARTHUR **EVERYTHING** YOU CHOOSE. I DO NOT CARE FOR MYSELF, BUT ALL FOR HIM!

I could see that she is somewhat bloodless, but I could not see the usual anaemic signs.

By chance she cut her hand slightly with broken glass. I secured a few drops of the blood and have analysed them.

The analysis gives a quite normal condition, and shows in itself a vigorous state of health. I have come to the conclusion that it must be something MENTAL.

48

Letter From Dr. Seward To Arthur Holmwood
(continued)

I have written to my old friend and master, Professor Van Helsing, of Amsterdam, who knows as much about obscure diseases as anyone in the world.

He is a seemingly arbitrary man, but this is because he knows what he is talking about better than anyone else. He is a philosopher and a metaphysician, and one of the most advanced scientists of his day; and he has, I believe, an absolutely open mind. This, with an iron nerve, a temper of the ice-brook, an indomitable resolution, self-command and toleration exalted from virtues to blessings, and the kindliest and truest heart that beats — these form his equipment for the noble work that he is doing for mankind.

I tell you these facts that you may know why I have such confidence in him. I have asked him to come at once.

Yours always,
John Seward.

Letter,
Abraham Van Helsing, M.D., D.Ph., D.Litt., etc., etc.
to Dr Seward

2 September.

My Good Friend —

When I received your letter I am already coming to you. By good fortune I can leave just at once, without wrong to any of those who have trusted me.

Have rooms for me at the Great Eastern Hotel, so that I may be near to hand, and please arrange that we may see the young lady not too late on tomorrow, for it is likely that I may have to return here that night.

But if need be I shall come again in three days, and stay longer if it must.

Till then good-bye, my friend John.

Van Helsing

PROFESSOR!

ARTHUR HOLMWOOD IS MY **FRIEND.** HE **TRUSTS** TO ME IN THIS MATTER.

YOU **MUST** TELL HIM **ALL** YOU THINK. TELL HIM WHAT **I** THINK, IF YOU CAN GUESS IT, IF YOU WILL.

NAY, I AM NOT **JESTING.** THIS IS **NO** JEST, BUT LIFE AND **DEATH,** PERHAPS MORE.

I asked what he meant by that, for he was very serious.

He would not give me any further clue.

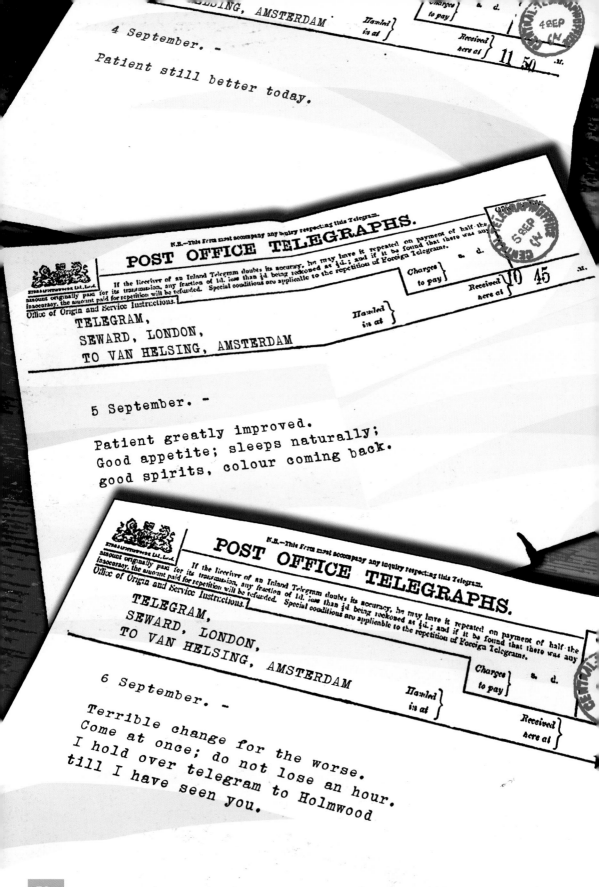

4 September. —

Patient still better today.

POST OFFICE TELEGRAPHS.

N.B.—This Form must accompany any inquiry respecting this Telegram.

If the receiver of an Inland Telegram doubts its accuracy, he may have it repeated on payment of half the amount originally paid for its transmission, any fraction of 1d. less than ½d. being reckoned as ½d.; and if it be found that there was any inaccuracy, the amount paid for repetition will be refunded. Special conditions are applicable to the repetition of Foreign Telegrams.
Office of Origin and Service Instructions.

Charges to pay   s.   d.

Received here at   10 45   .M.

TELEGRAM,
SEWARD, LONDON,
TO VAN HELSING, AMSTERDAM

Handed in at

5 September. —

Patient greatly improved.
Good appetite; sleeps naturally;
good spirits, colour coming back.

POST OFFICE TELEGRAPHS.

N.B.—This Form must accompany any inquiry respecting this Telegram.

If the receiver of an Inland Telegram doubts its accuracy, he may have it repeated on payment of half the amount originally paid for its transmission, any fraction of 1d. less than ½d. being reckoned as ½d.; and if it be found that there was any inaccuracy, the amount paid for repetition will be refunded. Special conditions are applicable to the repetition of Foreign Telegrams.
Office of Origin and Service Instructions.

TELEGRAM,
SEWARD, LONDON,
TO VAN HELSING, AMSTERDAM

Handed in at

Charges to pay   s.   d.

Received here at

6 September. —

Terrible change for the worse.
Come at once; do not lose an hour.
I hold over telegram to Holmwood
till I have seen you.

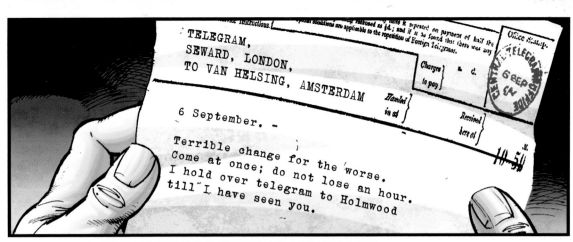

TELEGRAM,
SEWARD, LONDON,
TO VAN HELSING, AMSTERDAM

6 September. –

Terrible change for the worse.
Come at once; do not lose an hour.
I hold over telegram to Holmwood
till I have seen you.

CHAPTER TEN

LIVERPOOL STREET STATION, LONDON – 7 SEPTEMBER.

HAVE YOU SAID ANYTHING TO OUR YOUNG FRIEND THE LOVER OF HER?

NO. I WAITED TILL I HAD SEEN YOU. I WROTE HIM A LETTER SIMPLY TELLING HIM THAT YOU WERE COMING.

QUITE RIGHT! BETTER HE NOT KNOW AS YET; PERHAPS HE SHALL NEVER KNOW.

YOU DEAL WITH THE MADMEN. ALL MEN ARE MAD IN SOME WAY OR THE OTHER; AND AS YOU DEAL WITH YOUR MADMEN, SO DEAL WITH GOD'S MADMEN TOO – THE REST OF THE WORLD.

I HAVE FOR MYSELF THOUGHTS AT THE PRESENT. LATER I SHALL UNFOLD TO YOU.

WHY NOT NOW? IT MAY DO SOME GOOD; WE MAY ARRIVE AT SOME DECISION.

REMEMBER, MY FRIEND, THAT KNOWLEDGE IS STRONGER THAN MEMORY, AND WE SHOULD NOT TRUST THE WEAKER.

THIS CASE MAY BE OF SUCH INTEREST THAT ALL THE REST MAY NOT MAKE HIM KICK THE BEAM, AS YOUR PEOPLES SAY.

PUT DOWN IN RECORD EVEN YOUR DOUBTS AND SURMISES. WE LEARN FROM FAILURE, NOT FROM SUCCESS!

HILLINGHAM, NEAR LONDON.

Dr Seward's Diary
7 September. –
Mrs. Westenra met us. She was alarmed. I laid down a rule that she should not be present with Lucy or think of her illness more than was absolutely required. She assented. Van Helsing and I were shown up to Lucy's room.

She was ghastly, chalkily pale; her breathing was painful to see or hear.

MY GOD! THIS IS DREADFUL.

THERE IS **NO** TIME TO BE LOST. SHE WILL DIE FOR SHEER WANT OF **BLOOD** TO KEEP THE **HEART'S** ACTION AS IT SHOULD BE. THERE MUST BE **TRANSFUSION** OF BLOOD AT ONCE.

IS IT **YOU** OR **ME?**

I AM **YOUNGER** AND **STRONGER,** PROFESSOR. IT **MUST** BE ME.

THEN GET READY AT **ONCE.**

ARTHUR!

JACK, I WAS SO **ANXIOUS.**

I READ BETWEEN THE LINES OF YOUR LETTER, AND I HAVE BEEN IN AN **AGONY.**

SIR, YOU HAVE COME IN TIME. SHE IS **BAD,** VERY, **VERY** BAD. SHE WANTS **BLOOD** AND BLOOD SHE MUST **HAVE** OR DIE.

8 September. –
I sat up all night with Lucy. She never stirred, but slept on in a deep, health-giving sleep.

In the early morning her maid came, and I left her in her care and took myself home. A telegram came from Van Helsing that I should be at Hillingham tonight, and that he would join me early in the morning.

9 September. –
I was pretty tired and worn-out when I got to Hillingham. For two nights I had hardly had a wink of sleep.

NO SITTING UP TONIGHT FOR **YOU**. YOU ARE WORN-OUT. I AM QUITE **WELL** AGAIN.

I would not argue the point, but went and had my supper.

After supper, Lucy showed me a room next her own.

NOW YOU MUST STAY **HERE**. I SHALL LEAVE THIS DOOR **OPEN** AND MY DOOR TOO. IF I WANT **ANYTHING** I SHALL CALL OUT, AND YOU CAN COME TO ME AT ONCE.

So, on her renewing promise to call me if she should want anything, I lay on the sofa, and forgot about everything.

10 September. –
I was conscious of the Professor's hand on my head.

AND HOW IS OUR PATIENT?

WELL, WHEN I LEFT HER, OR RATHER WHEN **SHE** LEFT ME.

COME, LET US SEE.

GOTT IN HIMMEL!

QUICK! IT IS NOT TOO LATE. IT BEATS, THOUGH BUT FEEBLY. ALL OUR WORK IS UNDONE; WE MUST BEGIN AGAIN.

He produced the instruments for transfusion and, without a moment's delay, we began the operation.

DO NOT STIR, BUT I FEAR THAT WITH GROWING STRENGTH SHE MAY WAKE; AND THAT WOULD MAKE DANGER. BUT I SHALL GIVE INJECTION OF MORPHIA.

The effect on Lucy was not bad. I could see a faint tinge of colour steal back into the pallid cheeks and lips.

YOU TOOK A GREAT DEAL MORE FROM ART.

HE IS HER LOVER. YOU HAVE WORK TO DO FOR HER AND FOR OTHERS; AND THE PRESENT WILL SUFFICE. MIND, NOTHING MUST BE SAID OF THIS. IT WOULD AT ONCE FRIGHTEN AND ENJEALOUS HIM.

NOW, YOU GO HOME, AND EAT MUCH AND DRINK ENOUGH. MAKE YOURSELF STRONG. I STAY HERE TONIGHT, AND I SHALL SIT UP WITH LITTLE MISS MYSELF.

GOOD-NIGHT.

GOOD-NIGHT, PROFESSOR.

11 September. –
This afternoon I went over to Hillingham. Found Van Helsing in excellent spirits, and Lucy much better. She seemed quite unconscious that anything had happened.

WE OWE YOU **SO** MUCH, DR. SEWARD, FOR **ALL** YOU HAVE DONE, BUT YOU REALLY MUST NOW TAKE CARE NOT TO **OVERWORK** YOURSELF.

YOU ARE LOOKING **PALE** YOURSELF.

Shortly after I had arrived, a parcel from abroad came for the Professor.

THESE ARE FOR **YOU**, MISS LUCY.

FOR ME? OH, DR. VAN HELSING!

YES, MY DEAR, BUT NOT FOR YOU TO **PLAY** WITH. THESE ARE **MEDICINES**. I PUT HIM IN YOUR **WINDOW**, I MAKE PRETTY **WREATH**, AND HANG HIM ROUND YOUR **NECK**, SO THAT YOU SLEEP **WELL**.

OH YES! THEY, LIKE THE **LOTUS** FLOWER, MAKE YOUR TROUBLE **FORGOTTEN**.

OH, PROFESSOR, I BELIEVE YOU ARE ONLY PUTTING UP A **JOKE** ON ME. WHY, THESE FLOWERS ARE ONLY COMMON **GARLIC**!

FLING

NO **TRIFLING** WITH **ME**! I NEVER **JEST**! THERE IS GRIM **PURPOSE** IN ALL I DO. I ONLY DO FOR **YOUR** GOOD; BUT THERE IS MUCH **VIRTUE** TO YOU IN THOSE SO **COMMON** FLOWER.

WELL, PROFESSOR, I KNOW YOU ALWAYS HAVE A **REASON** FOR WHAT YOU DO, BUT A **SCEPTIC** WOULD SAY THAT YOU WERE WORKING SOME **SPELL** TO KEEP OUT AN **EVIL SPIRIT**.

PERHAPS I **AM**!

CHAPTER ELEVEN

13 September. –

Van Helsing and I arrived at Hillingham at eight o'clock. The bright sunshine and all the fresh feeling of early autumn seemed like the completion of nature's annual work.

When we arrived we met with Mrs. Westenra. She is always an early riser.

YOU WILL BE GLAD TO KNOW THAT LUCY IS **BETTER**. THE DEAR CHILD IS STILL **ASLEEP**.

AHA! I THOUGHT I HAD DIAGNOSED THE CASE. MY TREATMENT IS **WORKING**.

YOU MUST NOT TAKE ALL THE CREDIT TO **YOURSELF**, DOCTOR. LUCY'S STATE THIS MORNING IS DUE IN PART TO **ME**.

THERE WERE A LOT OF THOSE **HORRIBLE**, STRONG-SMELLING **FLOWERS** ABOUT **EVERYWHERE**, AND SHE HAD ACTUALLY A BUNCH OF THEM ROUND HER **NECK**.

THE HEAVY ODOUR WOULD BE TOO **MUCH** FOR THE DEAR CHILD IN HER **WEAK** STATE, SO I TOOK THEM ALL **AWAY** AND OPENED A BIT OF THE **WINDOW** TO LET IN A LITTLE **FRESH** AIR.

GOD! *GOD!* **GOD!**

THIS POOR MOTHER, ALL **UNKNOWING**, DOES SUCH THING AS **LOSE** HER DAUGHTER **BODY** AND **SOUL**; AND WE **MUST** NOT TELL HER, WE MUST NOT EVEN **WARN** HER, OR SHE **DIE**, AND THEN **BOTH** DIE.

OH, HOW WE ARE **BESET!** HOW ARE ALL THE POWERS OF THE **DEVILS** AGAINST US!

AS I **EXPECTED**. TODAY **YOU** MUST OPERATE. I SHALL PROVIDE. YOU ARE **WEAKENED** ALREADY.

Again the operation; again some return of colour to the ashy cheeks, and the regular breathing of healthy sleep. Van Helsing said he would watch this night and the next.

Lucy Westenrä's Diary
17 September. –
Four days and nights of peace. The noises that used to frighten me – the flapping against the windows, the distant voices, the harsh sounds that commanded me to do I know not what – have all ceased. I go to bed now without any fear of sleep. I have grown quite fond of the garlic.

Tonight Dr. Van Helsing is going away, but I need not be watched. Last night I awoke twice to find him asleep in his chair. I did not fear to go to sleep again, although the boughs or bats or something flapped almost angrily against the window-panes.

From The Pall Mall Gazette, 18 September

THE ESCAPED WOLF

Interview with the Keeper in the Zoological Gardens.

BERSICKER!

RRAAARRRH

That 'ere wolf that we called Bersicker never gave no trouble to talk of. But, there, you can't trust wolves.

When the animiles see us a-talkin' they lay down.

That there man kem over...

And with that he lifts his 'at as perlite as a lord, and walks away. Old Bersicker kep' a-lookin' arter 'im till 'e was out of sight, and then went and lay down in a corner, and wouldn't come hout the 'ole hevening.

SOON AS THE MOON WAS HUP, THE WOLVES ALL BEGAN A-'OWLING. THERE WARN'T **NOTHING** FOR THEM TO 'OWL **AT.**

JUST BEFORE TWELVE O'CLOCK I JUST TOOK A LOOK ROUND AFORE TURNIN' IN, BUT WHEN I KEM TO OLD BERSICKER'S CAGE, I SEE THE RAILS **BROKEN** AND **TWISTED** ABOUT AND THE CAGE **EMPTY.**

18 Sept.

Mall Gazette

THE ESCAPED WOLF

Interview with the Keeper in the Zoological Gardens.

DID ANYONE ELSE SEE **ANYTHING?** MR. BILDER, CAN YOU ACCOUNT IN ANY WAY FOR THE **ESCAPE** OF THE WOLF?

ONE OF OUR GARD'NERS SEES A BIG GREY **DOG** COMIN' OUT THROUGH THE GARDING 'EDGES BUT I DON'T GIVE **MUCH** FOR IT MYSELF.

IT SEEMS TO ME THAT 'ERE WOLF ESCAPED – SIMPLY BECAUSE HE **WANTED** TO GET **OUT.**

GOD **BLESS ME!** IF THERE AIN'T OLD BERSICKER COME **BACK** BY 'ISSELF!

The whole scene was an unutterable mixture of comedy and pathos. The wicked wolf that for half a day had paralysed London and set all children shivering in their shoes, was there in a penitent mood, and was received and petted like a sort of vulpine prodigal son.

I KNEW THE POOR OLD CHAP WOULD GET INTO SOME KIND OF TROUBLE. HERE'S HIS HEAD ALL CUT AND FULL OF BROKEN GLASS.

'E'S BEEN A-GETTIN' OVER SOME WALL OR OTHER, TOPPED WITH BROKEN BOTTLES. COME ALONG, BERSICKER.

Dr. Seward's Diary
17 September. –
I was engaged after dinner in my study posting up my books, which had fallen sadly into arrear.

Suddenly, in rushed my patient, his face distorted with passion. Without an instant's pause he made straight at me.

YAH!

He was too quick and too strong for me. Before I could get my balance he had struck at me.

Before he could strike again, however, I got in my RIGHT.

THWAK

When the attendants rushed in, he was LICKING UP like a dog, the BLOOD which had fallen from my wound.

THE BLOOD IS THE LIFE!

THE BLOOD IS THE LIFE!

Memorandum left by Lucy Westenra

17 September. Night.

I write this and leave it to be seen. I feel I am dying of weakness, and have barely strength to write, but it must be done if I die in the doing.

I went to bed as usual, taking care that the flowers were placed as Dr. Van Helsing directed, and soon fell asleep.

I was waked by the flapping at the window, which now I know so well. I feared to be alone, and called out.

flap flap flap

IS THERE ANYBODY THERE?

There was no answer. I was afraid to wake mother.

Outside I heard a sort of howl like a dog's, but more fierce and deeper. I went to the window...

flap flap flap

HOOOOWWL

...but could see nothing, except a big bat, so I went back to bed again, but determined not to go to sleep.

Presently the door opened, and mother came in.

I WAS UNEASY ABOUT YOU, DARLING, AND CAME IN TO SEE THAT YOU WERE ALL RIGHT.

YOU MIGHT CATCH COLD SITTING THERE, MOTHER. COME IN AND SLEEP WITH ME.

The flapping and buffeting came to the window again. After a while there was the low howl again.

HOOOOWWL

flap flap flap

WHAT IS THAT?

65

Her dear heart had ceased to beat. The sounds awoke the maids, who lifted the body of my dear mother, and laid her on the bed.

YOU ARE ALL SO **FRIGHTENED** AND **NERVOUS.** GO TO THE DINING-ROOM AND HAVE EACH A GLASS OF **WINE.**

I was surprised that the maids did not come back. I called them, but got no answer, so I went to the dining-room to look for them.

They lay helpless on the floor, breathing heavily. There was a queer, acrid smell about. I was suspicious, and examined the decanter. It smelt of laudanum.

WHAT AM I TO **DO?** I AM **ALONE,** SAVE FOR THE SLEEPING SERVANTS, WHOM SOMEONE HAS **DRUGGED.**

ALONE WITH THE **DEAD!** I DARE NOT GO **OUT,** FOR I CAN HEAR THE LOW HOWL OF THE **WOLF** THROUGH THE BROKEN WINDOW. GOD **SHIELD** ME FROM **HARM** THIS NIGHT!

I SHALL **HIDE** THIS PAPER IN MY **BREAST,** WHERE THEY SHALL **FIND** IT WHEN THEY COME TO LAY ME OUT. **GOOD-BYE,** DEAR ARTHUR, IF I SHOULD NOT **SURVIVE** THIS NIGHT.

AARRRRWHOOOOOOOO

GOD KEEP YOU, DEAR, AND GOD **HELP** ME!

CHAPTER TWELVE

Dr. Seward's Diary
18 September. –
I drove at once to Hillingham.
I could find no means of
ingress. Every window and
door was fastened and locked.

I met Van Helsing there.
Round the back of the house,
the Professor took a surgical
saw to the iron bars which
guarded the window.
We ascended to Lucy's room.

IT IS NOT YET TOO LATE!

QUICK! QUICK! BRING THE BRANDY! YOU GO WAKE THOSE MAIDS. FLICK THEM IN THE FACE WITH A WET TOWEL. MAKE THEM GET HEAT AND FIRE AND A WARM BATH.

SHE WILL NEED TO BE HEATED BEFORE WE CAN DO ANYTHING MORE.

THIS IS A STAND-UP FIGHT WITH DEATH.

IF THAT WERE ALL, I STOP HERE WHERE WE ARE NOW, AND LET HER FADE AWAY INTO PEACE, FOR I SEE NO LIGHT IN LIFE OVER HER HORIZON.

WE MUST HAVE ANOTHER TRANSFUSION OF BLOOD. WE ARE EXHAUSTED.

WHAT ARE WE TO DO FOR SOME ONE WHO WILL OPEN HIS VEINS FOR HER?

WHAT'S THE MATTER WITH ME, ANYHOW?

QUINCEY MORRIS!

WHAT BROUGHT YOU HERE?

I GUESS **ART** IS THE CAUSE.

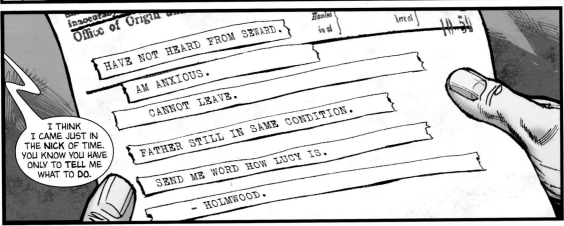

Office of Origin

HAVE NOT HEARD FROM SEWARD.

AM ANXIOUS.

CANNOT LEAVE.

FATHER STILL IN SAME CONDITION.

SEND ME WORD HOW LUCY IS.

— HOLMWOOD.

I THINK I CAME JUST IN THE **NICK** OF TIME. YOU KNOW YOU HAVE ONLY TO **TELL ME** WHAT TO **DO**.

A **BRAVE** MAN'S BLOOD IS THE **BEST** THING ON THIS EARTH WHEN A WOMAN IS IN **TROUBLE**.

WELL, THE **DEVIL** MAY WORK AGAINST US FOR ALL HE'S **WORTH**, BUT **GOD** SENDS US MEN WHEN WE **WANT** THEM.

Once again we went through that ghastly operation.

Her struggle back into LIFE was FRIGHTFUL to see and hear. However, the action of both heart and lungs improved, and Van Helsing made an injection of morphia, with good effect.

He handed me a sheet of note-paper that had fallen from Lucy's breast.

IN GOD'S NAME, WHAT DOES IT ALL **MEAN**?

DO NOT **TROUBLE** ABOUT IT **NOW**. YOU SHALL KNOW AND UNDERSTAND IT ALL IN GOOD TIME; BUT IT WILL BE LATER.

JACK SEWARD, I DON'T WANT TO SHOVE MYSELF ANYWHERE WHERE I'VE NO **RIGHT** TO BE; BUT THIS IS NO **ORDINARY** CASE.

THAT'S SO.

I TAKE IT THAT **BOTH** YOU AND VAN HELSING HAD DONE **ALREADY** WHAT I DID TODAY. AND I GUESS **ARTHUR** WAS THE **FIRST**; IS THAT NOT SO?

AND HOW **LONG** HAS THIS BEEN GOING ON?

ABOUT TEN DAYS.

TEN DAYS! THEN I GUESS THAT THAT POOR PRETTY CREATURE THAT WE **ALL** LOVE HAS HAD PUT INTO HER VEINS THE BLOOD OF **FOUR** STRONG MEN.

THAT IS THE **CRUX**. I CAN'T EVEN HAZARD A **GUESS**. BUT HERE WE **STAY** UNTIL ALL BE WELL – OR ILL.

WHAT TOOK IT **OUT?**

COUNT ME **IN**. YOU AND THE **DUTCHMAN** WILL TELL ME WHAT TO DO, AND I'LL DO IT.

When she woke late in the afternoon, Lucy realised to the full her mother's death. We tried what we could to comfort her, but she was very low in thought and spirit, and wept silently and weakly for a long time. Towards dusk she fell into a doze.

19 September. –
All last night she slept fitfully. The Professor and I took it in turns to watch. Quincey Morris patrolled round and round the house all night long.

In the afternoon she asked for Arthur. His presence acted as a stimulant, and she rallied a little.

Letter, Mina Harker to Lucy Westenra (unopened by her)

17 September.

My dearest Lucy, -

Well, I got my husband back all right. When we arrived at Exeter there was a carriage waiting for us, and in it, though he had an attack of gout, Mr. Hawkins. He took us to his own house, where there were rooms for us.

From my bedroom I can see the great elms of the cathedral close. Jonathan and Mr. Hawkins are busy all day; for, now that Jonathan is a partner, Mr. Hawkins wants to tell him all about the clients.

Letter, Mina Harker to Lucy Westenra (unopened by her)

18 September.

My dearest Lucy, -

Such a sad blow has befallen us. Mr. Hawkins has died very suddenly. We had come to so love him that it really seems as though we had lost a father. Jonathan feels deep sorrow for the dear, good man who has befriended him all his life, and now at the end has treated him like his own son and left him a fortune.

I dread coming up to London, as we must do, for poor Mr. Hawkins left in his will that he was to be buried in the grave with his father.

As there are no relations at all, Jonathan will have to be chief mourner. I shall try to run over to see you.

Forgive me for troubling you.

Good-bye, my dearest Lucy, and all blessings on you.

Your loving

Mina Harker

Their EYES met instead of their lips; and so they parted.

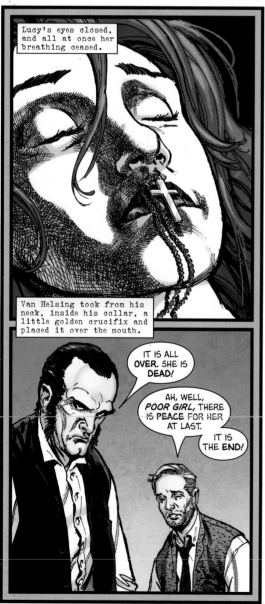

Lucy's eyes closed, and all at once her breathing ceased.

Van Helsing took from his neck, inside his collar, a little golden crucifix and placed it over the mouth.

IT IS ALL OVER. SHE IS DEAD!

AH, WELL, *POOR GIRL*, THERE IS PEACE FOR HER AT LAST.

IT IS THE END!

NOT *SO; ALAS!* NOT SO. IT IS ONLY THE BEGINNING!

BUT WE CAN DO NOTHING AS YET. WAIT AND SEE.

The funeral was arranged for the next succeeding day, so that Lucy and her mother might be buried together.

TOMORROW I WANT YOU TO BRING ME, BEFORE NIGHT, A SET OF POST-MORTEM KNIVES.

MUST WE MAKE AN AUTOPSY?

CHAPTER THIRTEEN

YES, AND NO. I WANT TO CUT OFF HER HEAD AND TAKE OUT HER HEART.

AH! YOU A SURGEON AND SO SHOCKED! WILL YOU NOT HAVE FAITH IN ME? I HAVE GOOD REASON NOW FOR ALL I WANT TO DO.

I -- I PROMISE.

Later that day, Van Helsing came into my room.

YOU NEED NOT TROUBLE ABOUT THE KNIVES; WE SHALL NOT DO IT.

WHY NOT?

BECAUSE IT IS TOO LATE. SEE! THIS CRUCIFIX WAS STOLEN IN THE NIGHT.

HOW STOLEN SINCE YOU HAVE IT NOW?

BECAUSE I GET IT BACK FROM THE WORTHLESS WRETCH WHO STOLE IT, FROM THE WOMAN WHO ROBBED THE DEAD AND THE LIVING.

HER PUNISHMENT WILL SURELY COME, BUT NOT THROUGH ME.

NOW WE MUST WAIT.

THERE WILL BE PAIN FOR US ALL.

I slept on a sofa in Arthur's room that night. Van Helsing did not go to bed at all. Lucy lay in her coffin, strewn with wild garlic flowers, which sent, through the odour of lily and rose, a heavy, overpowering smell into the night.

Mina Harker's Journal
22 September. –
Mr. Hawkins' funeral service was very simple and solemn. To take our minds off our sad loss, we walked down Piccadilly.

MY GOD!

JONATHAN! WHAT IS THE MATTER?

DO YOU SEE WHO IT IS? IT IS THE MAN HIMSELF!

I BELIEVE IT IS THE COUNT, BUT HE HAS GROWN YOUNG.

MY GOD, IF THIS BE SO! OH, MY GOD! IF I ONLY KNEW!

Later. – A sad home-coming in every way. A telegram from Van Helsing, whoever he may be...

TO MR. & MRS. HARKER

22 September. –

You will be grieved to hear that Mrs. Westenra died five days ago, and that Lucy died the day before yesterday.
They were both buried today.

Oh, what a wealth of sorrow in a few words!

76

THE WESTMINSTER GAZETTE

25 September.

A HAMPSTEAD MYSTERY

During the past two or three days several cases have occurred of young children straying from home or neglecting to return from their playing on the Heath. In all cases the children were too young to give any properly intelligible account of themselves, but the consensus of their excuses is that they had been with a "bloofer lady". On two occasions the children have not been found until early in the following morning.

Price One Penny.

THE WESTMINSTER GAZETTE

Some of the children, indeed all who have been missed at night, have been slightly torn or wounded in the throat. The wounds seem such as might be made by a rat or a small dog, and tends to show that whatever animal inflicts them has a system or method of its own. The police have been instructed to keep a sharp look-out for straying children, and for any stray dog.

CHAPTER FOURTEEN

Mina Harker's Journal
23 September. –

Jonathan is better after a bad night. My household work is done, so I shall take his foreign journal and read it...

POOR DEAR! HOW HE MUST HAVE **SUFFERED**, WHETHER IT BE **TRUE** OR ONLY **IMAGINATION**.

Letter,
Van Helsing to Mrs. Harker
24 September
(Confidence)

Dear Madam, --
I pray you to pardon my writing. I am empowered to read Miss Lucy Westenra's letters, which show how great friends you were and how you love her.

Oh, Madam Mina, by that love, I implore you, help me.

May it be that I see you? You can trust me.

Van Helsing.

Mina Harker's Journal
25 September. –

DR. VAN HELSING.

MRS. **HARKER**, IS IT NOT? MADAM MINA, IT IS ON ACCOUNT OF THE **DEAD** I COME.

SIR, YOU COULD HAVE NO **BETTER** CLAIM ON ME THAN THAT YOU WERE A **FRIEND** AND **HELPER** OF LUCY.

I KNOW THAT YOU WERE WITH LUCY AT **WHITBY**. SHE SOMETIMES KEPT A **DIARY**.

IN THAT DIARY SHE TRACES A **SLEEP-WALKING** IN WHICH YOU **SAVED** HER. I ASK YOU TO TELL ME ALL OF IT THAT YOU **REMEMBER**.

I WROTE IT ALL **DOWN** AT THE TIME.

READ IT OVER WHILST I ORDER LUNCH; AND THEN YOU CAN ASK ME **QUESTIONS** WHILST WE EAT.

OH, MADAM MINA, **HOW** CAN I SAY WHAT I **OWE** TO YOU? THIS PAPER IS AS **SUNSHINE**. IT OPENS THE **GATE** TO ME.

YOUR HUSBAND IS **NOBLE** NATURE, AND **YOU** ARE NOBLE TOO. AND YOUR HUSBAND – **TELL** ME OF HIM. IS HE QUITE **WELL**?

HE WAS ALMOST **RECOVERED**, BUT HE HAS BEEN GREATLY **UPSET** BY MR. HAWKINS' DEATH, FOR WHEN WE WERE IN **TOWN** HE HAD A SORT OF **SHOCK**.

HE THOUGHT HE **SAW** SOME ONE WHO RECALLED SOMETHING TERRIBLE, SOMETHING WHICH LED TO HIS **BRAIN FEVER**.

After breakfast I saw him to the station. His eye suddenly seemed to catch something in one of the London papers.

MEIN GOTT! *MEIN GOTT!* SO SOON! SO *SOON!*

Dr. Seward's Diary
26 September. -
Van Helsing came back today and thrust last night's "Westminster Gazette" into my hand.

WHAT DO YOU THINK OF *THAT?*

WESTMINSTER GA

No. 34

SEPTEMBER 2

A HAMPSTEAD MYSTERY

During the past two or three days several cases have occurred of young children straying from home or neglecting to return from their playing on the Heath. In all cases the children were too young to give any properly

intelligible account of themselves, but the consensus of excuses is that had been with "bloofer lady". On two occasions the children have not been found until early in the following morning.

Some of dren, have indeed al ght, been miss rn have been s e wounde s oat. The such as by a rat d tends

oke of York arrie

CHILDREN BEING DECOYED AWAY AT HAMPSTEAD... SMALL PUNCTURED WOUNDS ON THEIR THROATS...

...IT IS LIKE POOR **LUCY'S.** WHATEVER IT WAS THAT INJURED **HER** HAS INJURED **THEM.**

YOU ARE A CLEVER MAN, BUT YOU ARE TOO PREJUDICED. YOU DO NOT LET YOUR EYES SEE NOR YOUR EARS HEAR.

DO YOU NOT **THINK** THAT THERE ARE THINGS WHICH **YOU** CANNOT UNDERSTAND?

IN THE **PAMPAS** THERE ARE BATS THAT SUCK **DRY** THE VEINS OF **CATTLE** AND **HORSES** AT NIGHT. IN SOME ISLANDS OF THE **WESTERN SEAS** THERE ARE BATS THAT FLIT DOWN ON SLEEPING **SAILORS** ON DECK, AND THEN IN THE MORNING ARE FOUND **DEAD MEN.**

DO YOU MEAN TO TELL ME THAT **LUCY** WAS BITTEN BY SUCH A **BAT** HERE IN **LONDON?**

YOU THINK THEN THAT THOSE SO **SMALL** HOLES IN THE **CHILDREN'S** THROATS WERE MADE BY THE **SAME** THAT MADE THE HOLE IN MISS **LUCY?**

I SUPPOSE SO.

THEN YOU ARE *WRONG.* OH, WOULD IT WERE **SO!** IT IS FAR, **FAR** WORSE.

THEY WERE MADE BY MISS **LUCY!**

DR. VAN HELSING, ARE YOU *MAD?*

CHAPTER FIFTEEN

COME, I TELL YOU WHAT I PROPOSE: **FIRST,** THAT WE GO OFF NOW AND SEE THAT **CHILD** IN HOSPITAL. AND THEN WE SPEND THE NIGHT, YOU AND I, IN THE **CHURCHYARD** WHERE **LUCY** LIES.

THIS IS THE KEY THAT LOCK THE **TOMB.** I HAD IT FROM THE COFFIN-MAN TO GIVE TO **ARTHUR.**

My heart sank within me, for I felt that there was some fearful ORDEAL before us.

Our visit to the hospital took more time than we had reckoned on. There was no mistaking the similarity of the child's punctures to those which had been on Lucy's throat.

We dined at "Jack Straw's Castle" and about ten o'clock started from the inn. At last we reached the wall of the churchyard, which we climbed over.

With some difficulty - for it was very dark - we found the Westenra tomb.

27 September. –
Van Helsing insisted I go with him on another expedition. It was two o'clock before we found a suitable opportunity for our attempt.

ARE YOU CONVINCED NOW?

SEE, THEY ARE EVEN SHARPER THAN BEFORE. WITH THIS, THE LITTLE CHILDREN CAN BE BITTEN.

ARE YOU OF BELIEF NOW YOU HAVE SEEN THE COFFIN EMPTY LAST NIGHT, AND FULL TODAY?

SHE MAY HAVE BEEN PLACED HERE SINCE LAST NIGHT.

INDEED, YET SHE HAS BEEN DEAD ONE WEEK. MOST PEOPLES IN THAT TIME WOULD NOT LOOK SO.

SHE WAS BITTEN BY THE VAMPIRE WHEN IN A TRANCE.

WHEN THE UN-DEAD SLEEP, THEY GO BACK TO THE NOTHINGS OF THE COMMON DEAD, SO IT MAKE HARD THAT I MUST KILL HER IN HER SLEEP.

HOW WILL YOU DO THIS BLOODY WORK?

I SHALL CUT OFF HER HEAD AND FILL HER MOUTH WITH GARLIC, AND I SHALL DRIVE A STAKE THROUGH HER BODY.

IN TRANCE SHE DIED, AND IN TRANCE SHE UN-DEAD, TOO.

I waited a considerable time for Van Helsing to begin.

I HAVE BEEN THINKING, AND HAVE MADE UP MY MIND AS TO WHAT IS BEST. THERE ARE OTHER, MORE DIFFICULT THINGS TO FOLLOW;

WE MAY HAVE TO WANT ARTHUR, AND HOW SHALL WE TELL HIM OF THIS? HOW CAN I EXPECT HIM TO BELIEVE?

MY MIND IS MADE UP. LET US GO. WE FOUR SHALL RETURN TOMORROW NIGHT.

83

Note left by Van Helsing, directed to John Seward, M.D.

Tonight I go alone to watch in that churchyard.

It pleases me that the Un-Dead, Miss Lucy, shall not leave tonight; that so on the morrow night she may be more eager. Therefore I shall fix some things she like NOT -- garlic and a crucifix -- and so seal up the door of the tomb.

These are only to prevent her coming out; they may not prevail on her wanting to get in when she is desperate.

For Miss Lucy, or from her, I have no fear; but that other to whom is there that she is Un-Dead, he have now the power to seek her tomb and find shelter.

He is CUNNING; he has the strength of twenty men; even we four who gave our strength to Miss Lucy it also is all to him.

There is no reason why he should attempt the place. His hunting ground is more full of game than the churchyard where the Un-Dead woman sleep...

...and ONE old man watch.

Dr. Seward's Diary
28 September. –

MISS LUCY IS **DEAD**; IS IT NOT SO? BUT IF SHE BE **NOT DEAD** --

GOOD GOD! WHAT DO YOU MEAN? HAS SHE BEEN BURIED **ALIVE?**

I DID NOT SAY SHE WAS **ALIVE**. I GO NO FURTHER THAN TO SAY THAT SHE MIGHT BE *UN*-DEAD.

I WANT **YOUR** PERMISSION TO DO WHAT I THINK **GOOD** THIS NIGHT. MAY I **CUT OFF** THE **HEAD** OF DEAD MISS LUCY?

HEAVENS AND EARTH NO! NOT FOR THE WIDE WORLD WILL I CONSENT TO ANY **MUTILATION** OF HER DEAD BODY.

I HAVE A **DUTY** TO DO IN **PROTECTING** HER GRAVE FROM **OUTRAGE** AND, BY GOD I SHALL DO IT!

MY LORD GODALMING, I, **TOO**, HAVE A **DUTY** TO DO, A DUTY TO **OTHERS**, A DUTY TO **YOU**, A DUTY TO THE **DEAD**; AND, BY GOD, I SHALL DO IT!

ALL I ASK YOU NOW IS THAT YOU COME WITH ME, THAT YOU **LOOK** AND **LISTEN**. I SHALL DO MY DUTY, WHATEVER IT MAY SEEM TO ME.

BUT, I **BESEECH** YOU, DO NOT GO FORTH IN **ANGER** WITH ME. I HAVE **NEVER** HAD SO **HEAVY** A TASK AS NOW.

IF MY DEATH CAN DO HER **GOOD** EVEN NOW, WHEN SHE IS THE DEAD *UN*-DEAD, SHE SHALL HAVE IT **FREELY**.

OH, IT IS SO HARD TO **THINK** OF IT; BUT I WILL GO WITH YOU.

CHAPTER SIXTEEN

It was just a quarter before twelve o'clock when we got into the churchyard. Once more, the coffin was EMPTY! The Professor locked the door behind him and crumbled Catholic Sacred Wafer into the crevices between the door and its setting in the tomb...

SO THAT THE **UN-DEAD** MAY NOT **ENTER**.

We felt individually that in the presence of such earnest purpose as the Professor's, a purpose which could thus use the to him most sacred of things, it was impossible to distrust.

There was a long spell of silence, a big, aching void, and then...

S-S-S-S!

We saw a white figure advance, which held something dark at its breast.

My own heart grew cold as ice as we recognised the features of Lucy Westenra. Lucy Westenra, but how yet CHANGED.

=GASP=

We shuddered in horror.

Her eyes ranged over us, full of HELL-FIRE and blazed with UNHOLY light. She flung to the ground, callous as a devil, the child.

WAHAAAH'! AH! AHAH! WAAAAHH'!

THUD

We looked on in horrified amazement as we saw the woman, with a corporeal body as real at the moment as our own, pass in through the interstice where scarce a knife-blade could have gone.

COME NOW, MY FRIENDS; WE CAN DO NO MORE TILL **TOMORROW**. THERE IS A **FUNERAL** AT NOON, SO HERE WE SHALL ALL COME BEFORE LONG AFTER **THAT**. THEN THERE IS **MORE** TO DO.

THIS **LITTLE ONE** IS NOT MUCH **HARM**, AND BY TOMORROW SHALL BE **WELL**.

29 September, night. – We followed the Professor to the tomb.

IS THIS **REALLY LUCY'S** BODY, OR ONLY A **DEMON** IN HER **SHAPE?**

IT **IS** HER BODY, AND YET **NOT** IT. BUT **WAIT** A WHILE, AND YOU SHALL SEE HER AS SHE **WAS**, AND **IS.**

FOR **ALL** THAT **DIE** FROM THE **PREYING** OF THE UN-DEAD **BECOME** THEMSELVES UN-DEAD, AND **PREY** ON THEIR KIND –

NOSFERATU, AS THEY CALL IT IN EASTERN EUROPE.

THOSE **CHILDREN** WHOSE BLOOD SHE SUCK, BY HER **POWER** OVER THEM THEY **COME** TO HER.

BUT IF SHE **DIE** IN **TRUTH**, THEN ALL **CEASE**, AND THEY GO BACK TO THEIR PLAYS **UNKNOWING** EVER OF WHAT HAS BEEN.

WHEN THE **UN-DEAD** BECOME SUCH, THERE COMES WITH THE **CHANGE** THE CURSE OF **IMMORTALITY**; THEY CANNOT **DIE**, BUT MUST GO ON AGE AFTER AGE ADDING NEW VICTIMS AND MULTIPLYING THE **EVILS** OF THE WORLD;

MOST BLESSED OF ALL, WHEN THIS NOW UN-DEAD BE MADE TO **REST** AS **TRUE** DEAD, THEN THE **SOUL** OF THE POOR **LADY** WHOM WE LOVE SHALL AGAIN BE **FREE.** IT WILL BE A BLESSED **HAND** FOR HER THAT SHALL STRIKE THE **BLOW** THAT SETS HER FREE.

MY TRUE FRIEND, FROM THE **BOTTOM** OF MY **BROKEN** HEART I THANK YOU.

TELL ME WHAT I AM TO DO, AND I SHALL NOT **FALTER!**

BRAVE LAD! A MOMENT'S COURAGE, AND IT IS **DONE.** THIS **STAKE** MUST BE DRIVEN **THROUGH** HER.

TAKE IT IN YOUR LEFT HAND, READY TO PLACE TO THE POINT OVER THE **HEART,** AND THE **HAMMER** IN YOUR RIGHT.

THEN WHEN WE BEGIN OUR **PRAYER** FOR THE DEAD, **STRIKE** IN **GOD'S** NAME, THAT SO ALL MAY BE **WELL** WITH THE **DEAD** THAT WE **LOVE,** AND THAT THE **UN-DEAD** PASS **AWAY.**

Van Helsing opened his missal and began to read...

...then Arthur STRUCK with all his might.

AAAW

NEEEGH

89

Arthur bent and kissed her...

...and then we sent him and Quincey OUT of the tomb; the Professor and I sawed off the top of the stake. Then we cut off the head and filled the mouth with garlic.

Outside the air was sweet, the sun shone, and the birds sang, and it seemed as if all nature were tuned to a different pitch.

Dr. Seward's Diary

29 September. - morning.

Van Helsing received a telegram from Mina Harker. He told me I must meet her at Paddington Station, and got message to her en route, so that she may be prepared. He also gave me copies of the diaries she gave him.

DR. SEWARD, IS IT NOT?

AND YOU ARE MRS. HARKER!

I KNEW YOU FROM THE DESCRIPTION OF POOR DEAR LUCY, BUT --

She stopped suddenly, and a quick blush overspread her face.

29 September.- Carfax.

I had sent a wire to my housekeeper to have a sitting-room and bedroom prepared for Mrs. Harker. In due time we arrived. She knew, of course, that the place was a lunatic asylum, but I could see that she was unable to repress a slight shudder when we entered.

SHE TOLD ME THAT SHE WOULD COME PRESENTLY TO MY STUDY, SO HERE I AM FINISHING MY ENTRY IN MY PHONOGRAPH DIARY WHILST I AWAIT HER.

I HOPE I DID NOT KEEP YOU WAITING, BUT I STAYED AT THE DOOR AS I HEARD YOU TALKING, AND THOUGHT THERE WAS SOMEONE WITH YOU.

OH, I WAS ONLY ENTERING MY DIARY. I KEEP IT IN THIS.

WHY, THIS BEATS EVEN SHORTHAND! MAY I HEAR IT SAY SOMETHING?

YOU HELPED TO ATTEND DEAR LUCY AT THE END. LET ME HEAR HOW SHE DIED; FOR ALL THAT I KNOW OF HER, I SHALL BE VERY GRATEFUL. SHE WAS VERY, VERY DEAR TO ME.

TELL YOU OF HER DEATH? NOT FOR THE WIDE WORLD WOULD I LET YOU KNOW THAT TERRIBLE STORY.

BESIDES, I DO NOT KNOW HOW TO PICK OUT ANY PARTICULAR PART OF THE DIARY.

YOU DO NOT KNOW ME. WHEN YOU HAVE READ MY OWN DIARY AND MY HUSBAND'S ALSO, WHICH I HAVE TYPED, YOU WILL KNOW ME BETTER AND TRUST ME.

LET ME COPY YOUR DIARY OUT FOR YOU ON MY TYPEWRITER.

YOU ARE QUITE RIGHT. I DID NOT TRUST YOU, BUT I DO NOW. TAKE THE CYLINDERS AND HEAR THEM. DINNER WILL BY THEN BE READY.

CHAPTER SEVENTEEN

30 September. –
Mr. Harker arrived at nine o'clock. He is uncommonly clever and, if his journal be true, he is a man of great nerve. That going down to the vault a second time was a remarkable piece of daring.

He brought the letters of consignee of the boxes at Whitby and the carriers in London who took charge of them. Strange that it never struck me that the very next house might be the Count's hiding-place! Goodness knows that we had enough clues from the conduct of the patient Renfield.

I decided I should see Renfield, as hitherto he has been a sort of index to the coming and going of the Count. I found him sitting placidly. I am darkly suspicious. All those outbreaks were in some way linked with the proximity of the Count. What then does this absolute content mean?

DID YOU **TRACE** THAT **CARGO** OF THE **COUNT'S** FROM WHITBY TO **LONDON?**

I AM NOW **SATISFIED** THAT **ALL** THE BOXES WHICH ARRIVED AT WHITBY IN *THE DEMETER* WERE SAFELY DEPOSITED IN THE OLD **CHAPEL OF CARFAX.**

THERE SHOULD BE **FIFTY** THERE, UNLESS ANY HAVE BEEN **REMOVED.**

Mina Harker's Journal
30 September. –
Lord Godalming and Mr. Morris arrived earlier than we expected. Dr. Seward and Jonathan were out on business. It was to me a painful meeting, for it brought back all poor dear Lucy's hopes of only a few months ago.

I **LOVED** DEAR LUCY, AND I KNOW WHAT SHE WAS TO **YOU,** AND WHAT YOU WERE TO HER.

SHE AND I WERE LIKE **SISTERS;** AND NOW SHE IS **GONE,** WILL YOU NOT LET ME BE LIKE A SISTER TO **YOU** IN YOUR TROUBLE? FOR **LUCY'S** SAKE?

I KNOW NOW HOW I **SUFFERED,** BUT I DO NOT KNOW EVEN YET HOW MUCH YOUR SWEET SYMPATHY HAS BEEN TO ME TODAY. I SHALL KNOW **BETTER** IN TIME.

YOU WILL LET ME BE LIKE A **BROTHER,** WILL YOU NOT, FOR DEAR **LUCY'S** SAKE?

FOR DEAR LUCY'S SAKE. I PROMISE.

I THINK IT **GOOD** THAT I TELL YOU SOMETHING OF THE **KIND** OF ENEMY WITH WHICH WE HAVE TO DEAL. THERE **ARE** SUCH THINGS AS **VAMPIRES**; SOME OF US HAVE **EVIDENCE** THAT THEY **EXIST**. THE TEACHINGS AND THE RECORDS OF THE **PAST** GIVE PROOF **ENOUGH**. WE **MUST** WORK, THAT **OTHER** SOULS PERISH **NOT**, WHILST WE CAN **SAVE**.

THE **NOSFERATU** DO NOT **DIE** LIKE THE **BEE** WHEN HE STING ONCE. HE IS ONLY **STRONGER**, AND BEING **STRONGER**, HAVE YET **MORE** POWER TO WORK EVIL. HE CAN APPEAR AT WILL IN MANY FORMS, DIRECT THE **ELEMENTS** AND **COMMAND** ALL THE MEANER THINGS: THE **RAT**, THE **BAT**, AND THE **WOLF**; HE CAN AT TIMES **VANISH**.

WE ARE FACE TO FACE WITH **DUTY**. MUST WE **SHRINK**? I SAY **NO**. WHAT SAY **YOU**?

COUNT ME **IN**, PROFESSOR!

I AM **WITH** YOU.

BANG

THE VAMPIRE IS KNOWN EVERYWHERE THAT **MEN** HAVE BEEN. IN OLD **GREECE**, IN OLD **ROME**; HE FLOURISH IN **GERMANY**, **FRANCE**, **INDIA**, AND IN **CHINA**.

HE HAVE **FOLLOW** THE WAKE OF THE **BERSERKER** ICELANDER, THE DEVIL-BEGOTTEN **HUN**, THE **SLAV**, THE **SAXON**, THE **MAGYAR**. THE VAMPIRE **LIVE ON**, AND CANNOT DIE BY MERE PASSING OF THE **TIME**; HE CAN **FLOURISH** WHEN THAT HE CAN FATTEN ON THE **BLOOD** OF THE **LIVING**.

EVEN **MORE**, WE HAVE SEEN AMONGST US THAT HE CAN EVEN GROW **YOUNGER**. BUT HE CANNOT FLOURISH **WITHOUT** THIS DIET; HE EAT **NOT** AS OTHERS. HE THROWS NO **SHADOW**; HE MAKE IN THE MIRROR NO **REFLECT**!

HE HAS THE **STRENGTH** OF **MANY**. HE CAN TRANSFORM TO **WOLF**; HE CAN BE AS **BAT**. HE CAN COME IN **MIST** WHICH HE CREATE, BUT THE DISTANCE IS LIMITED. HE COME ON **MOONLIGHT** RAYS AS ELEMENTAL AS **DUST**.

HE CAN, WHEN ONCE HE FIND HIS **WAY**, COME **OUT** FROM ANYTHING OR **INTO** ANYTHING.

HE CAN DO **ALL** THESE THINGS, YET HE IS NOT **FREE**. HE CANNOT GO WHERE HE LISTS. HE MAY NOT ENTER **ANYWHERE** AT THE FIRST, UNLESS SOMEONE **BID** HIM TO COME; THOUGH AFTERWARDS HE CAN COME AS HE **PLEASE**.

HIS POWER **CEASES**, AS DOES THAT OF **ALL** EVIL THINGS, AT THE COMING OF THE **DAY**. IF HE BE **NOT** AT THE PLACE WHITHER HE IS **BOUND**, HE CAN ONLY CHANGE HIMSELF AT **NOON** OR AT EXACT **SUNRISE** OR **SUNSET**.

THERE ARE THINGS THAT **AFFLICT** HIM THAT HE HAS **NO** POWER: THE **GARLIC** AND THE **CRUCIFIX**. THERE ARE **OTHERS**, TOO: A BRANCH OF **WILD ROSE** ON HIS COFFIN; A **SACRED BULLET** FIRED INTO THE COFFIN; AND AS FOR THE **STAKE** THROUGH HIM, WE KNOW **ALREADY** OF ITS **PEACE**; OR THE CUT OFF **HEAD** THAT GIVETH **REST**.

BUT HE IS **CLEVER**. I ASK MY FRIEND AT BUDA-PESTH UNIVERSITY, WHO TELL ME HE MUST HAVE BEEN THAT *VOIVODE DRACULA* WHO WON HIS NAME AGAINST THE **TURK**.

IF IT BE SO, THEN WAS HE NO **COMMON** MAN; HE WAS SPOKEN OF AS THE **CLEVEREST**, MOST **CUNNING**, AND **BRAVEST** OF THE SONS OF THE *"LAND BEYOND THE FOREST"*.

THAT **MIGHTY** BRAIN AND IRON RESOLUTION WENT WITH HIM TO HIS **GRAVE**, AND ARE EVEN NOW ARRAYED **AGAINST** US. THE **DRACULAS** WERE A GREAT AND **NOBLE** RACE, THOUGH WERE HELD TO HAVE HAD **DEALINGS** WITH THE *EVIL ONE*.

95

AND NOW WE MUST **SETTLE** WHAT WE DO. WE HAVE HERE **MUCH** DATA, AND WE MUST PROCEED TO LAY OUT OUR **CAMPAIGN.**

WE KNOW THAT FROM THE CASTLE TO WHITBY CAME FIFTY BOXES OF **EARTH,** ALL OF WHICH WERE DELIVERED AT **CARFAX;** SOME OF THESE BOXES HAVE BEEN **REMOVED.**

WE MUST **TRACE** EACH OF THESE BOXES; AND WHEN WE ARE READY, WE MUST EITHER **CAPTURE** OR **KILL** THIS MONSTER IN HIS **LAIR;** OR WE MUST **STERILISE** THE EARTH, SO THAT NO MORE HE CAN SEEK **SAFETY** IN IT.

WE MAY FIND HIM IN HIS FORM OF **MAN** BETWEEN THE HOURS OF **NOON** AND **SUNSET,** AND SO **ENGAGE** WITH HIM WHEN HE IS AT HIS MOST **WEAK.**

AND NOW FOR **YOU,** MADAM MINA, THIS NIGHT IS THE **END** UNTIL ALL BE **WELL.** YOU ARE TOO **PRECIOUS** TO US TO HAVE SUCH **RISK.**

WHEN WE PART TONIGHT, YOU NO MORE MUST **QUESTION.** WE SHALL ACT ALL THE MORE **FREE** THAT YOU ARE NOT IN THE **DANGER,** SUCH AS **WE** ARE.

AS THERE IS NO TIME TO **LOSE,** I VOTE WE HAVE A LOOK IN HIS HOUSE **RIGHT** NOW.

TIME IS **EVERYTHING** WITH HIM; AND **SWIFT** ACTION ON OUR PART MAY **SAVE** ANOTHER **VICTIM.**

1 October.—
Just as we were about to leave...

RENFIELD WANTS TO SEE YOU AT **ONCE,** DR. SEWARD. I HAVE NEVER SEEN HIM SO **EAGER.** IF YOU DON'T SEE HIM **SOON,** HE WILL HAVE ONE OF HIS VIOLENT **FITS.**

ALL RIGHT; I'LL GO **NOW.**

MAY I COME **ALSO?**

ME TOO?

CHAPTER NINETEEN

Jonathan Harker's Journal

1 October, 5 a.m. –

I went with the party to the search with an easy mind, for I never saw Mina so well. I am glad she consented to hold back. We were, I think, all a little upset by the scene with Mr. Renfield.

MY FRIENDS, WE ARE GOING INTO **TERRIBLE** DANGER, AND WE NEED ARMS OF **MANY** KINDS.

OUR ENEMY IS NOT MERELY **SPIRITUAL**; HE HAS THE **STRENGTH** OF **TWENTY** MEN. WE MUST, THEREFORE, **GUARD** OURSELVES FROM HIS **TOUCH**. KEEP THIS NEAR YOUR **HEART**.

He lifted a little silver crucifix and held it out to me.

The professor crossed himself as he passed over the threshold. I could not get away from the feeling that there was someone else amongst us. I think the feeling was common to us all.

YOU **KNOW** THIS PLACE, JONATHAN. YOU HAVE **COPIED MAPS** OF IT, AND YOU KNOW AT LEAST MORE THAN **WE** DO. WHICH IS THE **WAY** TO THE **CHAPEL?**

I HAVE AN **IDEA** OF ITS **DIRECTION**, THOUGH ON MY FORMER VISIT I HAD NOT BEEN ABLE TO GET **ADMISSION** TO IT.

I led the way, and after a few wrong turnings...

THIS IS THE SPOT.

The long disuse had made the air stagnant and foul, with an odour composed of all the ills of mortality with the pungent, acrid smell of blood.

FAUGH! EVERY **BREATH** EXHALED BY THAT MONSTER **CLINGS** TO THE PLACE!

For a moment or two we stood appalled, all save Lord Godalming, who was seemingly prepared for such an emergency. He swung the door open and blew a low, shrill call.

It was answered from behind Dr. Seward's house by the yelping of dogs...

Squee Squee Squee

...and after about a minute...

GRARR

RRAR

Squee Squee Squee

The dogs rushed at their natural enemies. They fled; the whole mass vanished.

RARR

ROWF

Squee

Squeee

Squeeee

GRRARR

With their going it seemed as if some evil presence had departed. We all seemed to find our spirits rise.

We began our search of the house. We found nothing throughout except dust, all untouched from my first visit.

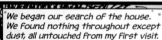

SO BE IT THAT HE HAS GONE ELSEWHERE. GOOD! IT HAS GIVEN US AN OPPORTUNITY TO CRY "CHECK" IN THIS CHESS GAME, WHICH WE PLAY FOR THE STAKE OF HUMAN SOULS.

AND NOW LET US GO HOME.

We all overslept, for the day was a busy one, and the night had no rest at all. Even Mina must have felt its exhaustion – I was awake before her and had to call two or three times before she awoke. She looks paler than usual.

Mina Harker's Journal

1 October. –

Last night I went to bed when the men had gone, full of devouring anxiety. I can't quite remember how I fell asleep. I remember hearing the sudden barking of the dogs and a lot of queer sounds, like praying on a tumultuous scale, from Mr. Renfield's room.

The mist was spreading, lying thick against the wall, as though it were stealing up to the windows. The poor man was more loud than ever.

AAARRRGH!

NO!

AAARRRRRGHHH!

GRARR RRAR SQUEE SQUEE SQUEE

And then there was silence. Not a thing seemed to be stirring, but all to be grim and fixed as death; so that a thin streak of white mist, that crept slowly across the grass, seemed to have a sentience and vitality all its own.

I was so frightened that I crept into bed. I was not then a bit sleepy, but I must have fallen asleep.

I was powerless to act; my feet, and my hands, and my brain were weighted. My dream was very peculiar.

The fog had grown thicker and poured into the room. I closed my eyes, but could still see through my eyelids. In my dream I must have fainted, for all became black darkness. The last conscious effort which imagination made was to show me a livid white face bending over me out of the mist.

2 October, 10 p.m. –

Last night I slept; but did not dream. I must have slept soundly, for I was not waked by Jonathan coming to bed; but the sleep has not refreshed me, for today I feel terribly weak and spiritless.

I hope I have not done wrong, for a new fear comes: that I may have been foolish in thus depriving myself of the power of waking.

I must be careful of such dreams, for they would unseat one's reason if there were too much of them.

CHAPTER TWENTY

Jonathan Harker's Journal
1 October. –

I FOUND A WORKMAN WHO REMEMBERED ALL ABOUT THE INCIDENT OF THE BOXES, AND HE WAS ABLE TO TELL ME THE DESTINATIONS.

HE TOOK SIX TO MILE END NEW TOWN, SIX TO BERMONDSEY, AND NINE TO A DUSTY OLD HOUSE IN PICCADILLY.

HOW DID HE GET INTO THE HOUSE?

HE SAID THE PARTY THAT ENGAGED HIM WAS AT THE HOUSE.

HE HAD HELPED THEM LOAD THE BOXES FROM CARFAX, TOO – THE "STRONGEST CHAP" HE'D EVER SEEN.

ALTHOUGH THIS WORKMAN COULDN'T REMEMBER THE NUMBER OF THE HOUSE, HE TOLD ME WHERE IT WAS.

THIS HAS BEEN A GREAT DAY'S WORK, FRIEND JONATHAN. DOUBTLESS WE ARE ON THE TRACK OF THE MISSING BOXES.

IF WE FIND THEM ALL IN THAT HOUSE, THEN OUR WORK IS NEAR THE END.

SAY! HOW ARE WE GOING TO GET INTO THAT HOUSE?

WE GOT INTO THE OTHER.

BUT, ART, THIS IS DIFFERENT. WE BROKE HOUSE AT CARFAX, BUT WE HAD NIGHT AND A WALLED PARK TO PROTECT US.

IT WILL BE A MIGHTY DIFFERENT THING TO COMMIT BURGLARY IN PICCADILLY, EITHER BY DAY OR NIGHT.

As nothing could well be done before morning, we decided not to take any active step before breakfast time.

Mina sleeps soundly and her breathing is regular. She is still too pale.

Tomorrow will, I hope, mend all this; she will be herself at home in Exeter. Oh, but I am sleepy!

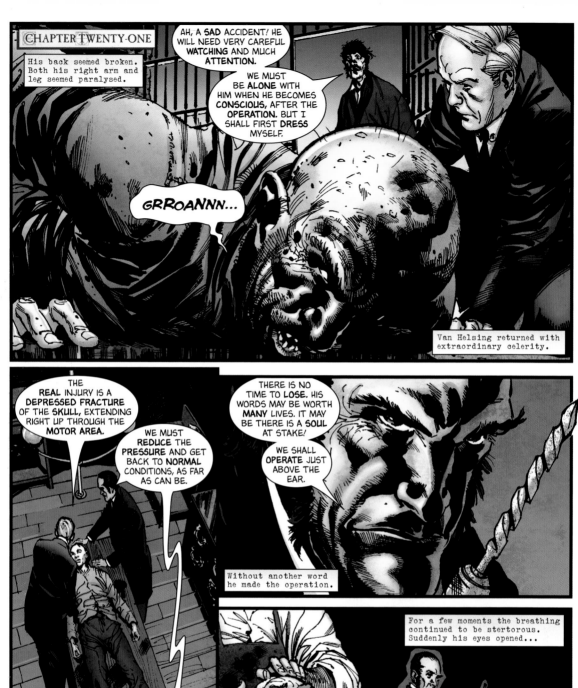

CHAPTER TWENTY-ONE

His back seemed broken. Both his right arm and leg seemed paralysed.

AH, A SAD ACCIDENT! HE WILL NEED VERY CAREFUL *WATCHING* AND MUCH *ATTENTION.*

WE MUST BE *ALONE* WITH HIM WHEN HE BECOMES *CONSCIOUS,* AFTER THE OPERATION. BUT I SHALL FIRST *DRESS* MYSELF.

GRROANNN...

Van Helsing returned with extraordinary celerity.

THE *REAL* INJURY IS A *DEPRESSED* FRACTURE OF THE *SKULL,* EXTENDING RIGHT UP THROUGH THE *MOTOR AREA.*

WE MUST *REDUCE* THE *PRESSURE* AND GET BACK TO *NORMAL* CONDITIONS, AS FAR AS CAN BE.

THERE IS NO TIME TO *LOSE.* HIS WORDS MAY BE WORTH *MANY* LIVES. IT MAY BE THERE IS A *SOUL* AT STAKE!

WE SHALL *OPERATE* JUST ABOVE THE *EAR.*

Without another word he made the operation.

THE *SUFFUSION* OF THE BRAIN WILL INCREASE *QUICKLY,* SO WE MUST *TREPHINE* AT ONCE OR IT MAY BE TOO *LATE.*

The patient was sinking fast. He might die at any moment.

For a few moments the breathing continued to be stertorous. Suddenly his eyes opened...

DOCTOR, I AM *DYING!*

I FEEL THAT I HAVE BUT A FEW *MINUTES;* AND THEN I MUST GO BACK TO *DEATH* -- OR *WORSE!*

I HAVE SOMETHING THAT I *MUST* SAY BEFORE I DIE; OR BEFORE MY POOR CRUSHED *BRAIN* DIES ANYHOW.

ALL DAY I *WAITED* TO *HEAR* FROM HIM, BUT HE DID NOT SEND ME *ANYTHING*, NOT EVEN A BLOW-FLY, AND WHEN THE MOON GOT UP I WAS PRETTY *ANGRY* WITH HIM.

HE *SLID* IN THROUGH THE *WINDOW*. HE *SNEERED* AT ME, AND HE WENT ON AS THOUGH HE *OWNED* THE WHOLE PLACE, AND *I* WAS NO ONE.

"HE DIDN'T EVEN *SMELL* THE SAME AS HE WENT BY ME. I COULDN'T *HOLD* HIM. I THOUGHT THAT, SOMEHOW, *MRS. HARKER* HAD COME INTO THE ROOM."

WHEN MRS. HARKER CAME IN TO SEE ME THIS AFTERNOON SHE WASN'T THE *SAME*; IT WAS LIKE TEA AFTER THE TEAPOT HAD BEEN *WATERED*. SHE DIDN'T *LOOK* THE SAME.

I DON'T *CARE* FOR THE *PALE* PEOPLE, I LIKE THEM WITH *LOTS* OF BLOOD IN THEM, AND *HERS* HAD ALL SEEMED TO HAVE *RUN OUT*.

"WHEN SHE WENT AWAY, I BEGAN TO *THINK*, AND IT MADE ME *MAD* TO KNOW THAT HE HAD BEEN TAKING THE *LIFE* OUT OF HER."

"SO WHEN HE CAME *TONIGHT* I WAS *READY* FOR HIM. I SAW THE MIST STEALING IN, AND I GRABBED IT TIGHT."

"I THOUGHT I WAS GOING TO *WIN*, FOR I DIDN'T MEAN HIM TO TAKE ANY *MORE* OF HER LIFE, TILL I SAW HIS *EYES*."

"THEY BURNED INTO ME, AND MY STRENGTH BECAME LIKE WATER."

"WHEN I TRIED TO CLING TO HIM, HE RAISED ME UP AND FLUNG ME DOWN."

"THERE WAS A RED CLOUD BEFORE ME, AND A NOISE LIKE THUNDER, AND THE MIST SEEMED TO STEAL AWAY UNDER THE DOOR."

FWAM

WE KNOW THE WORST NOW. HE IS HERE, AND WE KNOW HIS PURPOSE. IT MAY NOT BE TOO LATE.

LET US BE ARMED – THE SAME AS WE WERE THE OTHER NIGHT, BUT LOSE NO TIME; THERE IS NOT AN INSTANT TO SPARE.

We gathered outside the Harkers' door.

SHOULD WE DISTURB HER? MAY IT NOT FRIGHTEN HER TERRIBLY? IT'S UNUSUAL TO BREAK INTO A LADY'S ROOM!

YOU ARE ALWAYS RIGHT;

BUT THIS IS LIFE AND DEATH.

WHEN I TURN THE HANDLE, MY FRIENDS, YOU PUT YOUR SHOULDER DOWN AND SHOVE.

107

NOW!

KRAAASH

I felt my hair rise like bristles on the back of my neck, and my heart seemed to stand still.

HISSSS!

With a wrench, which threw his victim back upon the bed, he turned and SPRANG at us.

Lifting our crucifixes, he cowered, just as poor Lucy had done outside the tomb.

HISSSS!

BLAM BLAM

The moonlight suddenly failed as a black cloud sailed across the sky, and the faint vapour trailed away.

By this time, Mrs. Harker had drawn her breath and with it had given a SCREAM so wild, so ear-piercing, so despairing that it will ring in my ears till my DYING DAY.

NEEEEAAAAARRGH

AND **NOW**, POOR, DEAR MADAM MINA, TELL US **EXACTLY** WHAT HAPPENED. I DO NOT WANT THAT YOU BE **PAINED**, BUT IT IS NEED THAT WE KNOW **ALL**.

I FELT THE SAME VAGUE **TERROR** WHICH HAD COME TO ME **BEFORE**, AND THE SAME PRESENCE.

I TURNED TO JONATHAN, BUT I COULD NOT **WAKE** HIM. THIS CAUSED ME **GREAT** FEAR.

"BESIDE THE BED STOOD A **MAN**. I **KNEW** HIM FROM YOUR DESCRIPTIONS. I WOULD HAVE SCREAMED OUT, ONLY THAT I WAS **PARALYSED**..."

SILENCE! IF YOU MAKE A **SOUND** I SHALL DASH HIS **BRAINS** OUT BEFORE YOUR VERY **EYES**.

FIRST, A LITTLE **REFRESHMENT** TO REWARD MY EXERTIONS.

YOU MAY AS WELL BE **QUIET**; IT IS NOT THE **FIRST** TIME, OR THE **SECOND**, THAT **YOUR** VEINS HAVE APPEASED MY **THIRST!**

AND SO **YOU**, LIKE THE OTHERS, WOULD PLAY **YOUR** BRAINS AGAINST **MINE**.

WHILST THEY PLAYED **WITS** AGAINST ME -- AGAINST **ME** WHO COMMANDED NATIONS, AND FOUGHT FOR THEM, **HUNDREDS** OF YEARS BEFORE THEY WERE **BORN** -- I WAS **COUNTERMINING** THEM.

AND **YOU**, THEIR **BEST** BELOVED ONE, ARE NOW TO **ME**, FLESH OF **MY** FLESH; BLOOD OF **MY** BLOOD; MY **BEAUTIFUL** WINE-PRESS FOR A WHILE...

YOU WOULD HELP THESE MEN TO **HUNT** ME AND **FRUSTRATE** MY DESIGNS!

THEY WILL KNOW IN **FULL** BEFORE LONG WHAT IT IS TO CROSS **MY** PATH.

... AND SHALL BE LATER ON MY **COMPANION** AND MY **HELPER**.

BUT AS YET YOU ARE TO BE **PUNISHED** FOR WHAT YOU HAVE DONE. YOU HAVE AIDED IN **THWARTING** ME; NOW YOU SHALL **COME** TO **MY** CALL.

WHEN MY **BRAIN** SAYS "COME!" TO YOU, YOU SHALL CROSS **LAND** OR **SEA** TO DO MY BIDDING.

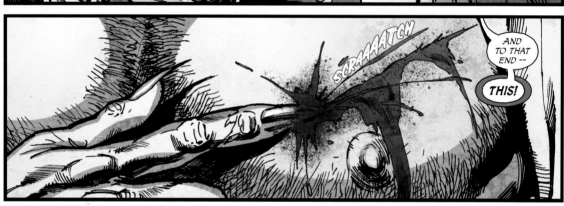

SCRAAAAATCH

AND TO THAT END --

THIS!

"HE SEIZED MY NECK AND PRESSED MY **MOUTH** TO THE **WOUND,** SO THAT I MUST EITHER **SUFFOCATE** OR **SWALLOW** SOME OF THE --"

-- OH, MY GOD, MY **GOD!** WHAT HAVE I **DONE** TO DESERVE SUCH A **FATE,** I WHO HAVE TRIED TO WALK IN MEEKNESS AND **RIGHTEOUSNESS** ALL MY DAYS?

GOD **PITY** ME!

As she was telling her terrible story, the eastern sky began to quicken.

Harker was still and quiet; but over his face came a grey look which deepened and deepened in the morning light.

112

CHAPTER TWENTY-TWO

Jonathan Harker's Journal
3 October. –

Dr. Van Helsing and Dr. Seward found Renfield lying on the floor, all in a heap. His face was bruised, and the bones of the neck were broken. The attendant confessed to dozing, but had heard Renfield calling out "God!" several times. After that there was a sound of falling.

THERE MUST BE NO MORE **CONCEALMENT**. ALAS! WE HAVE HAD TOO **MUCH** ALREADY. BESIDES, NOTHING CAN GIVE ME **MORE** PAIN THAN I HAVE ALREADY ENDURED.

BUT DEAR **MADAM MINA**, ARE YOU NOT **AFRAID**; NOT FOR YOURSELF, BUT FOR OTHERS **FROM** YOURSELF?

AH **NO!** IF I FIND IN MYSELF A SIGN OF HARM TO **ANY** THAT I LOVE, I SHALL **DIE!**

YOU MUST NOT DIE BY **ANY** HAND, BUT LEAST OF ALL BY YOUR **OWN**. UNTIL THE **OTHER**, WHO HAS **FOULED** YOUR SWEET LIFE, IS **TRUE DEAD** YOU MUST **NOT** DIE;

FOR IF **HE** IS STILL **UN-DEAD**, YOUR DEATH WOULD MAKE **YOU** EVEN AS **HE** IS.

NO, YOU MUST **LIVE!**

IF GOD WILL LET ME LIVE, I WILL **STRIVE** TO DO SO.

IT IS **WELL** THAT WE DECIDED **NOT** TO DO ANYTHING WITH THE **EARTH-BOXES** IN CARFAX. NOW, THE COUNT DOES NOT KNOW OUR **INTENTIONS**. IN ALL PROBABILITY, HE DOES NOT KNOW THAT SUCH A POWER **EXISTS** TO US AS CAN STERILISE HIS **LAIRS**. WHEN WE HAVE EXAMINED THE HOUSE IN **PICCADILLY**, WE MAY TRACK THE VERY **LAST** OF THEM.

TODAY, THEN, IS **OURS**. THE **SUN** THAT ROSE ON OUR SORROW THIS MORNING **GUARDS** US IN ITS COURSE. UNTIL IT **SETS** TONIGHT, THAT MONSTER MUST **RETAIN** WHATEVER FORM HE NOW HAS. AND SO WE HAVE THIS DAY TO **HUNT OUT** ALL HIS LAIRS AND **STERILISE** THEM.

THEN LET US COME AT **ONCE**; WE ARE **WASTING** PRECIOUS TIME! WE SHALL **BREAK INTO** THAT HOUSE IN PICCADILLY IF NEED BE.

AND YOUR **POLICE**? WHERE WILL **THEY** BE, AND WHAT WILL THEY **SAY**?

WE SHALL GO AFTER TEN O'CLOCK WITH A **LOCKSMITH**, AS IF WE WERE **OWNERS** OF THE HOUSE.

It was agreed that before starting for Piccadilly we should destroy the Count's lair close at hand.

NOW, MY DEAR FRIENDS, WE GO **FORTH** TO OUR TERRIBLE ENTERPRISE. MADAM MINA, YOU ARE QUITE SAFE **HERE** UNTIL THE **SUNSET**; AND **BEFORE** THEN WE SHALL RETURN -- IF WE **SHALL RETURN**!

BUT **BEFORE** WE GO LET ME SEE YOU **ARMED** AGAINST PERSONAL ATTACK. LET ME **GUARD** YOURSELF.

ON YOUR **FOREHEAD** I TOUCH THIS PIECE OF **SACRED WAFER** IN THE NAME OF THE **FATHER**, THE **SON**, AND --

AAAHH!

UNCLEAN! I AM **UNCLEAN!**

YOU MAY HAVE TO **BEAR** THAT **MARK** TILL GOD **HIMSELF** SEE FIT TO **LIFT** THE BURDEN THAT IS HARD UPON US.

IT MAY BE THAT WE **ASCEND** TO HIS BIDDING THROUGH **TEARS** AND **BLOOD**; THROUGH **DOUBTS** AND **FEARS**, AND ALL THAT MAKES THE **DIFFERENCE** BETWEEN GOD AND **MAN**.

There was hope in his words, and comfort.

I said farewell to Mina, and we entered Carfax without trouble and found all things the same as the first occasion. The earth smelled musty.

WE MUST **STERILISE** THIS EARTH.

HE **CHOSE** THIS EARTH BECAUSE IT HAS BEEN **HOLY**. THUS WE **DEFEAT** HIM WITH HIS **OWN** WEAPON, FOR WE MAKE IT **MORE** HOLY STILL; WE **SANCTIFY** IT TO GOD.

Taking from his box a Sacred Wafer, the Professor laid it reverently on the earth, and then shut the lid and screwed it home. One by one we treated in the same way each of the great boxes; in each was a portion of the Host.

Our work in Carfax done, we caught the train to Piccadilly.

Lord Godalming found a locksmith to gain entry to the house in Piccadilly. Not a soul took the slightest notice.

In the dining-room, we found eight boxes of earth. Eight boxes only out of the nine which we sought! Our work was not over, and would never be until we should have found the missing box. We opened them, one by one, and treated them as we had treated those in the old chapel.

CHAPTER TWENTY-THREE

It was evident to us that the Count was not present, and we proceeded to search for any of his effects. There were title-deeds of the Piccadilly house, and of houses at Mile End and Bermondsey.

Lord Godalming and Quincey took accurate notes of the addresses, took with them a little heap of keys that were there, and set out to destroy the boxes in these places.

Dr. Seward's Diary
3 October. -
Harker is overwhelmed in misery. Last night we was full of energy with dark brown hair. Today, he is a drawn and haggard man, whose white hair matches well with the hollow burning eyes and grief-written lines of his face.

His energy is still intact; in fact he is a living flame. This may yet be his salvation.

We were startled by a knock at the hall door. It was the double postman's knock of the telegraph boy, who handed Van Helsing a despatch.

"LOOK OUT FOR D. HE HAS JUST NOW, 12.45, COME FROM CARFAX. HE SEEMS TO BE GOING THE ROUND AND MAY WANT TO SEE YOU. – MINA."

NOW, GOD BE **THANKED**, WE SHALL SOON MEET. I CARE FOR **NOTHING** NOW, EXCEPT TO **WIPE OUT** THIS **BRUTE** FROM THE FACE OF **CREATION**.

I WOULD SELL MY **SOUL** TO DO IT!

Half an hour later, Lord Godalming and Quincey Morris returned.

IT IS ALL RIGHT. WE FOUND **BOTH** PLACES; **SIX** BOXES IN EACH, AND WE **DESTROYED** THEM ALL!

THERE'S NOTHING TO DO BUT WAIT **HERE**. IF, HOWEVER, HE DOESN'T TURN UP BY FIVE O'CLOCK, WE **MUST** START OFF; FOR IT WON'T DO TO LEAVE MRS. HARKER **ALONE** AFTER SUNSET.

HE WILL BE **HERE** BEFORE LONG NOW.

We could hear a key softly inserted in the lock of the hall door.

chchik

Hush! Have all your arms! Be ready!

With a swift glance round the room, Quincey at once laid out our plan of attack, and without speaking a word, with a gesture, placed us each in position.

clump clump

We waited in suspense. The slow, careful steps came along the hall.

The Count was evidently prepared for some surprise – at least he feared it.

Suddenly with a single bound he leaped into the room, winning a way past us before any of us could raise a hand to stay him.

There was something so panther-like in the movement, something so UNHUMAN, that it seemed to sober us all from the shock.

It was a pity that we had not some better organised plan of attack, for even at the moment I wondered what we were to do.

Harker evidently meant to try the matter and made a fierce and sudden cut at him. The quickness of the Count's leap back saved him.

swiiijsh

The expression of the Count's face was so hellish, that for a moment I feared for Harker.

Instinctively I moved forward with a protective impulse, holding the crucifix. I felt a mighty POWER fly along my arm.

YOU THINK TO **BAFFLE** ME, YOU ~ WITH YOUR PALE FACES ALL IN A **ROW**, LIKE **SHEEP** IN A **BUTCHER'S**.

YOU SHALL BE **SORRY** YET, EACH ONE OF YOU! YOU THINK YOU HAVE LEFT ME WITHOUT A PLACE OF **REST**; BUT I HAVE **MORE**. MY REVENGE IS *JUST BEGUN!*

BAH!

SKAAAAAAAAASH

I SPREAD IT OVER **CENTURIES**, AND TIME IS ON **MY** SIDE.

YOUR GIRLS THAT YOU **LOVE** ARE **MINE** ALREADY; AND THROUGH THEM YOU AND OTHERS SHALL **YET BE MINE** ~ **MY** CREATURES, TO DO **MY** BIDDING AND TO BE **MY** JACKALS WHEN I WANT TO **FEED**.

YOU FOLLOW **QUICK!** YOU ARE **HUNTERS** OF WILD **BEAST!**

They rushed into the yard to follow the Count, but there was no sign of him.

LET US GO **BACK** TO POOR, DEAR MADAM MINA. ALL WE CAN DO JUST NOW IS **DONE**; AND WE CAN THERE, AT LEAST, **PROTECT** HER.

BUT WE NEED NOT **DESPAIR**. THERE IS BUT **ONE** MORE EARTH-BOX, AND WE MUST TRY TO **FIND** IT. WHEN THAT IS DONE ALL MAY YET BE **WELL**.

With sad hearts we came back to my house.

Jonathan Harker's Journal
4 October, morning. –

JONATHAN DEAR, I WANT YOU TO BEAR SOMETHING IN **MIND** THROUGH ALL THIS **DREADFUL** TIME. IT IS NOT A WORK OF **HATE**. THAT POOR SOUL WHO **WROUGHT** ALL THIS **MISERY** IS THE SADDEST CASE OF **ALL**. YOU MUST BE **PITIFUL** TO HIM, THOUGH IT MAY NOT HOLD YOUR HANDS FROM HIS **DESTRUCTION**.

IF I COULD SEND HIS SOUL FOR EVER TO BURNING **HELL** I WOULD **DO** IT!

OH, **HUSH!** IN THE NAME OF THE GOOD GOD. DON'T **SAY** SUCH THINGS. PERHAPS... SOME DAY... I **TOO** MAY NEED SUCH **PITY**.

I HAVE AN IDEA. THE PROFESSOR MUST HYPNOTISE ME BEFORE THE DAWN, AND THEN I SHALL BE ABLE TO SPEAK.

WHERE ARE YOU?

I DO NOT KNOW. SLEEP HAS NO PLACE IT CAN CALL ITS OWN. IT IS ALL STRANGE TO ME! IT IS ALL DARK.

THEN YOU ARE ON A SHIP?

OH, YES! THERE IS THE SOUND OF MEN STAMPING OVERHEAD; THE CREAKING OF A CHAIN; THE CHECK OF THE CAPSTAN FALLING INTO THE RATCHET.

WHAT DO YOU HEAR?

THE LAPPING WATER. LITTLE WAVES LEAP. I CAN HEAR THEM ON THE OUTSIDE.

I AM STILL -- OH, SO STILL. IT IS LIKE DEATH!

GO QUICK, DEAREST; THE TIME IS GETTING CLOSE.

Van Helsing stopped and Mina awoke after a few moments' sleep.

IT MAY NOT BE YET TOO LATE! THAT SHIP WAS WEIGHING ANCHOR WHILST SHE SPOKE.

THE COUNT SAW THAT WITH BUT ONE EARTH-BOX LEFT, AND A PACK OF MEN FOLLOWING LIKE DOGS AFTER A FOX, LONDON WAS NO PLACE FOR HIM, AND HE LEAVE THE LAND.

HE THINK TO ESCAPE, BUT NO! WE FOLLOW HIM! NOW MORE THAN EVER MUST WE FIND HIM EVEN IF WE HAVE TO FOLLOW HIM TO THE JAWS OF HELL!

HE, OUR ENEMY, HAVE GONE AWAY. HE HAVE GONE BACK TO HIS CASTLE IN TRANSYLVANIA. I FELT SURE HE MUST GO BY THE DANUBE MOUTH, OR BY SOMEWHERE IN THE BLACK SEA. WE FIND THAT ONLY ONE BLACK SEA BOUND SHIP GO OUT WITH THE TIDE, AND SHE IS THE CZARINA CATHERINE, AND SHE SAIL FOR VARNA.

CHAPTER TWENTY-FOUR

5 October. –

WE INQUIRE OF THE GOINGS OF THE CZARINA CATHERINE.

A TALL MAN, THIN AND PALE, WITH TEETH SO WHITE AND BURNING EYES ASK THAT THE CAPTAIN COME TO HIM. HE GIVE MUCH TALK TO THE CAPTAIN AS TO HOW AND WHERE HIS BOX IS TO BE PLACE.

AND SO, OUR ENEMY IS ON THE SEA, WITH THE FOG AT HIS COMMAND.

WE KNOW ALL ABOUT **WHERE** HE GO, FOR WE HAVE SEEN THE **OWNER** OF THE SHIP. TO SAIL A SHIP TAKES **TIME.** WE GO ON **LAND** MORE **QUICK,** AND WE **MEET** HIM THERE.

OUR **BEST** HOPE IS TO COME ON HIM WHEN IN THE **BOX** BETWEEN **SUNRISE** AND **SUNSET;** FOR THEN HE CAN MAKE NO **STRUGGLE.**

WE SHALL BE IN VARNA A DAY **BEFORE** THE SHIP ARRIVES.

IS IT REALLY **NECESSARY** TO PURSUE THE COUNT? SINCE HE HAS BEEN **DRIVEN** FROM ENGLAND, WILL HE NOT **AVOID** IT?

IT **IS** NECESSARY! FOR **YOUR** SAKE, AND FOR THE SAKE OF **HUMANITY.** HE COME **AGAIN,** AND **AGAIN.** HIS GLIMPSE THAT HE HAVE HAD, **WHET** HIS APPETITE ONLY AND ENKEEN HIS **DESIRE.**

I UNDERSTAND THAT THE COUNT COMES FROM **WOLF** COUNTRY. I PROPOSE THAT WE ADD **WINCHESTERS** TO OUR ARMAMENT.

GOOD! WINCHESTERS IT SHALL BE.

YOU **MUST** TAKE ME **WITH** YOU! I AM **SAFER** WITH YOU, AND **YOU** SHALL BE SAFER TOO.

BUT **WHY,** DEAR MADAM MINA?

YOU **KNOW** THAT **YOUR** SAFETY IS OUR **SOLEMNEST** DUTY.

MADAM MINA, YOU ARE, AS ALWAYS, MOST **WISE.** YOU **SHALL** WITH US COME.

IN THE MORNING WE SHALL LEAVE FOR **VARNA.**

WHEN THE COUNT **WILLS** ME I MUST GO. IF HE TELLS ME TO COME IN **SECRET,** I MUST COME BY **ANY** DEVICE TO HOODWINK – EVEN **JONATHAN.**

YOU MEN ARE **BRAVE** AND **STRONG.** YOU ARE STRONG IN YOUR **NUMBERS.** BESIDES, I MAY OF SERVICE, SINCE YOU CAN **HYPNOTISE** ME AND SO LEARN THAT WHICH EVEN I **MYSELF** DO NOT **KNOW.**

Jonathan Harker's Journal

15 October. Varna. –

We left Charing Cross on the morning of the 12th, got to Paris the same night, and took the places secured for us in the Orient Express. We travelled night and day, arriving here at about five o'clock.

Mina is well, and looks to be getting stronger; her colour is coming back. She sleeps a great deal; throughout this journey she slept nearly all the time. Before sunrise and sunset, however, she is very wakeful and alert; and it has become a habit for Van Helsing to hypnotise her at such times.

He always asks her what she can see and hear. It is evident that the Czarina Catherine is still at sea, hastening on her way to Varna.

Tomorrow we are to see the Vice-Consul, and to arrange about getting on board the ship as soon as she arrives. Van Helsing says that our chance will be to get on board between sunrise and sunset.

The Count, even if he takes the form of a bat, cannot cross the running water of his own volition, and so cannot leave the ship.

As he dare not change to man's form without suspicion, he must remain in the box. If, then, we can come on board after sunrise, he is at our mercy; for we can open the box and make sure of him, as we did of poor Lucy, before he wakes.

What mercy he will get from us will not count for much.

We think we shall not have much trouble with officials. Thank God! This is the country where bribery can do anything, and we are well supplied with money.

16 October. –
Mina's report still the same: lapping waves, rushing water and favourable winds.

We have arranged with certain officials that the instant the Czarina Catherine is seen to pass the Dardanelles, we are to be informed by a special messenger.

Dr. Seward's Diary
24 October. –
A whole week of waiting. Then a telegram to Godalming told us that the Czarina Catherine had reached the Dardanelles.

She should therefore arrive here some time in the morning.

25 October. –
No news yet of the ship's arrival.

26 October. –
Another day and no tidings. She ought to be here by now.

27 October. –
No news yet of the ship we wait for. Mrs. Harker reported as usual.

Lapping waves and rushing water. The waves are very faint.

124

28 October. —

When the telegram came announcing the arrival of the Czarina Catherine in Galatz, I do not think it was such a shock to any of us. We did not know when the bolt would come, but we expected something.

LET US **ORGANISE.** FRIEND ARTHUR, GET THE **TRAIN** TICKETS FOR US TO GO TO **GALATZ** IN THE MORNING.

JONATHAN, GO TO THE AGENT OF THE SHIP AND GET AUTHORITY TO MAKE **SEARCH** JUST AS IT WAS **HERE.**

QUINCY MORRIS, **YOU** SEE THE VICE-CONSUL TO MAKE OUR WAY **SMOOTH** TO GALATZ.

My Friend, in the trance of three days ago the **Count** sent Mina his **spirit** to read her **mind.** He **learn** then that we are **here.** Now he make his most effort to **escape** us.

She knows it **not,** and it would **overwhelm** her just when we want **all** her **hope** and **courage.**

Oh, John, my friend, we are in **awful** straits. I **fear,** as I **never** feared before.

We can **only** trust the good God.

125

Chapter Twenty-Six

Dr. Seward's Diary
29 October. —
Last night we all assembled a little before the time of sunset. When the usual time came round Mrs. Harker prepared herself for her hypnotic effort.

I can see **nothing**; we are **still**; there are **no** waves lapping, but only a steady **swirl** of water softly running against the hawser. I can hear men's **voices** calling, and the tramping of **feet**.

What is **this?**

There is a gleam of **light**; I can feel the **air** blowing upon me.

Suddenly she sat up and opened her eyes.

WOULD NONE OF YOU LIKE A CUP OF **TEA?** YOU MUST ALL BE SO **TIRED!**

YOU SEE, MY FRIENDS. HE IS **CLOSE** TO LAND; HE HAS LEFT HIS EARTH-CHEST. BUT HE HAS YET TO GET ON **SHORE.**

HE CAN, IF IT BE IN THE **NIGHT,** CHANGE HIS FORM AND CAN **JUMP** OR **FLY** ON SHORE, AS HE DID AT **WHITBY.**

BUT IF THE DAY COME **BEFORE** HE GET ON SHORE, THEN, UNLESS HE BE **CARRIED** HE CANNOT **ESCAPE.**

AND IF HE BE **CARRIED,** THEN THE **CUSTOMS** MAY DISCOVER WHAT THE BOX **CONTAINS.** IF HE ESCAPE NOT ON SHORE **TONIGHT,** WE MAY THEN ARRIVE IN **TIME.**

And so it is that we are travelling towards Galatz in an agony of expectation.

30 October, 7.a.m. —
We are near Galatz now.

All is **dark.** Men talking in **strange** tongues. I hear lapping **water,** level with me, and the **creaking** of wood on wood. **Cattle** low far off.

Galatz.

Mina Harker's Journal

30 October. –

Mr. Morris took me to the hotel where our rooms had been ordered by telegraph. Lord Godalming went to the Vice-Consul, as his rank might serve as a guarantee of some sort to the official. Jonathan and the two doctors went to the shipping agent to learn particulars of the arrival of the Czarina Catherine.

Jonathan Harker's Journal

30 October. –

On board the Czarina Catherine with Captain Donelson...

IT'S NO **CANNY** TO RUN FRAE LONDON TO THE BLACK SEA WI' A WIND AS THOUGH THE **DEIL HIMSELF** WERE BLAWIN' ON YER SAIL FOR HIS **AIN** PURPOSE.

A **FOG** FELL ON US AND TRAVELLED WI' US. WHEN WE GOT PAST THE BOSPHORUS THE MEN BEGAN TO **GRUMBLE;** THE ROUMANIANS ASKED ME TO HEAVE **OVERBOARD** A BIG **BOX** PUT ON BOARD BY A QUEER-LOOKIN' **OLD MAN** JUST BEFORE WE HAD STARTED FRAE **LONDON.**

I HAD SEEN THEM PUT OUT THEIR TWA **FINGERS** WHEN THEY **SAW** HIM, TO GUARD AGAINST THE **EVIL EYE.** MAN! THEIR SUPERSTEETIONS! I SENT THEM ABOOT THEIR **BUSINESS.**

THE FOG CLOSED IN ON US AND DIDN'T LET UP FOR **FIVE** DAYS.

WHEN THE MORNING **SUN** CAME THROUGH THE FOG, WE FOUND OURSELVES JUST IN THE RIVER OPPOSITE **GALATZ.**

THE ROUMANIANS HAD TAKEN THE BOX ON **DECK** READY TO FLING **IN.** I HAD TO **ARGY** WI' THEM ABOOT IT WI' A **HANDSPIKE.**

PROPERTY WERE BETTER IN **MY** HANDS THAN IN THE **DANUBE.**

IN THE MORNIN', A MAN CAME ABOORD WI' AN **ORDER** TO RECEIVE A BOX MARKED FOR ONE **COUNT DRACULA.** GLAD I WAS TO BE **RID** O' THE DAM' THING.

We later met the man who took the box from the ship. He told us it was given in charge to a certain Petrof Skinsky, who dealt with the Slovaks who traded down the river to the port.

When we sought for Skinsky, one of his neighbours told us that his body had been found inside the churchyard of St. Peter.

The throat had been torn open as if by some wild animal.

Mina Harker's Journal
30 October, evening. –
They were so tired and dispirited, I asked them to lie down for half an hour.

After they had rested I got our party together for them to judge my conclusion.

MY SURMISE IS **THIS**: WHEN THE BOX WAS ON **LAND**, BEFORE SUNRISE OR AFTER SUNSET, HE CAME OUT FROM HIS **BOX**, MET SKINSKY AND INSTRUCTED HIM WHAT TO DO AS TO ARRANGING THE **CARRIAGE** OF THE BOX UP SOME **RIVER** IN AN **OPEN BOAT**.

WHEN THIS WAS **DONE**, AND HE KNEW THAT ALL WAS IN **TRAIN**, HE BLOTTED OUT HIS **TRACES**, AS HE THOUGHT, BY **MURDERING** HIS AGENT.

I HAVE EXAMINED THE **MAP** AND FIND THAT THE RIVER MOST **SUITABLE** FOR THE SLOVAKS TO HAVE ASCENDED IS THE **SERETH**, JOINED BY THE **BISTRITZA** --

-- WHICH RUNS UP THE **BORGO PASS**, AS **CLOSE** TO **DRACULA'S CASTLE** AS CAN BE GOT BY **WATER**.

I SHALL GET A **STEAM LAUNCH** AND FOLLOW HIM.

AND I, **HORSES** TO FOLLOW ON THE **BANK** LEST BY CHANCE HE **LAND**. I HAVE BROUGHT SOME **WINCHESTERS**; THEY ARE PRETTY **HANDY** IN A CROWD, AND THERE MAY BE **WOLVES**.

YOU MUST NOT BE **ALONE**, ART.

I THINK **I** HAD BETTER GO WITH **QUINCEY**. WE HAVE HUNTED TOGETHER, AND WILL BE A MATCH FOR **WHATEVER** MAY COME ALONG.

FRIEND **JONATHAN**, BE **NOT** AFRAID FOR MADAM MINA. SHE WILL BE MY **CARE**.

YOU GO WITH LORD GODALMING IN THE STEAM-BOAT UP THE **RIVER**, WHILE I WILL TAKE MADAM MINA RIGHT INTO THE **HEART** OF THE ENEMY'S COUNTRY.

DO YOU MEAN TO BRING MINA RIGHT INTO THE **JAWS** OF HIS **DEATH-TRAP?** NOT FOR THE WORLD!

NOT FOR **HEAVEN** OR **HELL!**

HAVE YOU **SEEN** THAT AWFUL DEN OF HELLISH INFAMY? HAVE **YOU** FELT THE VAMPIRE'S LIPS UPON YOUR **THROAT?**

OH MY FRIEND, IT IS BECAUSE I WOULD **SAVE** MADAM MINA FROM THAT AWFUL PLACE THAT I WOULD **GO**.

GOD **FORBID** THAT I SHOULD TAKE HER **INTO** THAT PLACE!

DO AS YOU **WILL**. WE ARE IN THE HANDS OF GOD!

Mina Harker's Journal

30 October, Later. –

We shall drive ourselves, for we have no one whom we can trust in the matter. We have all got arms, even for me a large-bore revolver.

Alas I cannot carry __one__ *arm like the rest do; the scar on my forehead forbids that.*

It took all my courage to say good-bye to my darling Jonathan. We may never meet again. Courage, Mina! There must be no tears now – unless it may be that God will let them fall in gladness.

Jonathan Harker's Journal

October 30, night. –

I am writing this in the light of the furnace door of the steam launch; Lord Godalming is firing up. He is an experienced hand at the work, as he has had launches of his own on the Thames and the Norfolk Broads.

As we are rushing through the darkness on the Bistritza, with the cold seeming to rise up and strike us, we seem to be drifting into a whole world of dark and dreadful things.

Dr. Seward's Diary

2 November. –

Three days on the road. We have had only the rest needful for the horses; but we are both bearing it wonderfully. We must push on.

4 November. –

Today we heard of the launch having been detained by an accident when trying to force a way up the rapids. The Slovak boats get up all right, by aid of a rope, and steering with knowledge. Godalming is an amateur fitter himself, and evidently he put the launch in trim again.

CHAPTER TWENTY-SEVEN

Mina Harker's Journal

2 November, night. –

All day long driving. The country gets wilder as we go, and the great spurs of the Carpathians seem to gather round us and tower in front. We both seem in good spirits.

Memorandum by Abraham Van Helsing

4 November. --

This is to my old and true friend John Seward, M.D., in case I may not see him. It is so cold that the grey heavy sky is full of snow. It seems to have affected Madam Mina. She sleeps, and sleeps, and sleeps! We got to the Borgo Pass just after sunrise yesterday morning.

In hypnotic sleep, as before, Madam Mina answered, "Darkness and the swirling of water".

WELL, IF IT BE THAT SHE SLEEP ALL THE *DAY*, IT SHALL ALSO BE THAT I DO *NOT* SLEEP AT NIGHT.

5 November, morning. –
All yesterday we travel, moving into a more and more wild and desert land.

Ere the great dark came upon us, I make a fire. I got ready food: but she would not eat, saying that she had not hunger.

Then, with the fear on me of what might be, I drew a large ring around us; and over the ring I passed some of the Wafer, and I broke it fine so that all was well guarded.

Madam Mina could not cross the ring; then none of those we dreaded could.

Presently the horses began to scream, and tore at their tethers till I came to them and quieted them. The snow flakes and the mist began to circle round, till I could get a shadowy glimpse of those women that would have kissed Jonathan.

I turned to Madam Mina:

HERE YOU ARE *SAFE!*

HA HA HA!

FEAR FOR ME! WHY FEAR FOR ME? NONE SAFER IN ALL THE **WORLD** FROM **THEM** THAN I AM!

The figures came closer, but keeping ever without the Holy circle.

COME, SISTER. COME TO US. COME!

COME!

GOD BE THANKED MADAM MINA IS NOT, YET, OF THEM.

Holding out some of the Wafer, I advanced on them.

HISSS!

They could not approach me, whilst so armed, nor Madam Mina whilst she remained in the ring, which she could not leave no more than they could enter.

And so we remained until the red of the dawn began to fall through the snow-gloom. The horrid figures melted in the whirling mist and snow; the wreaths of transparent gloom moved away towards the castle.

I have seen the horses; they are all dead.

I am at least sane. Thank God for that mercy at all events. When I left Madam Mina sleeping within the Holy circle, I took my way to the castle. Jonathan's bitter experience served me here.

By memory of his diary I found my way to the old chapel, for I knew that here my work lay. The air was oppressive; it seemed as if there was some sulphurous fume, which made me dizzy.

I knew that there were at least three graves to find -- graves that are inhabit; so I search and search, and I find one of them.

She lay in her Vampire sleep, so full of life and voluptuous beauty.

Then the beautiful eyes of the fair woman open and look love -- many a man would find his nerve fail him at such things.

I was moved to a yearning for delay which seemed to paralyse my faculties and clog my very soul. Before the spell could be wrought further upon me, I had nerved myself to my wild work.

AAAIEEEGH

133

It was butcher work. The horrid screeching... but it is over! And the poor souls, I can pity them now and weep.

Hardly had my knife severed the head of each, before the whole body began to melt away and crumble into its native dust, as though the death that should have come centuries agone had at last assert himself.

Before I left the castle I so fixed its entrances that never more can the Count enter there Un-Dead.

Madam Mina awoke from her sleep when I returned to her.

COME AWAY FROM THIS AWFUL PLACE! LET US GO TO MEET MY HUSBAND WHO IS, I KNOW, COMING TOWARDS US.

And so with trust and hope, yet full of fear, we go eastward to meet our friends -- and him -- whom Madam Mina tell me that she know are coming to meet us.

Mina Harker's Journal

6 November. -

When we had gone about a mile, I was tired with the heavy walking. We could hear the distant howling of wolves. They were far off, but the sound was full of terror. Dr. Van Helsing sought some strategic point, where we would be less exposed in case of attack.

In a little while the Professor found a wonderful spot.

HERE YOU WILL BE IN SHELTER; AND IF THE WOLVES DO COME I CAN MEET THEM ONE BY ONE.

LOOK! MADAM MINA, LOOK!

Straight in front of us and not far off came a group of men with a cart. On the cart was a great square chest. My heart leaped as I saw it, for I felt the end was coming.

The evening was now drawing close, when the Thing would take new freedom and could in any of many forms elude all pursuit.

LOOK! LOOK! SEE, TWO HORSEMEN FOLLOW FAST, COMING UP FROM THE SOUTH.

IT MUST BE QUINCEY AND JOHN.

Looking around I saw on the north side two other men, riding at break-neck speed. One of them I knew was Jonathan, and the other I took to be Lord Godalming. They were all converging.

HALT!

HALT!

135

The leader of the gipsies, in a fierce voice, gave a word at which every man drew what weapon he carried, and held himself in readiness to attack. Issue was joined in an instant.

All four men of our party threw themselves from their horses and dashed towards the cart. Jonathan and Quincey were bent on finishing their task before the sun should set.

BLAM

THOK

Jonathan's impetuosity, and the manifest singleness of his purpose, seemed to overawe those in front of him; instinctively they cowered aside and let him pass.

In an instant he had jumped upon the cart, and...

THWAK

...with a strength that seemed incredible...

GNNYAAGH!

THUD

...raised the great box and flung it over the wheel to the ground.

SHLK

Mr. Morris had had to use force to pass through his side of the ring of Szgany. I saw the knives of the gipsies flash as he won a way through them, and they cut at him.

At first I thought that he too had come through in safety...

URLLLGHHHH!

...but as he sprang beside Jonathan, I could see that he was clutching at his side.

SCREEEECH!

He did not delay notwithstanding this. Under the efforts of both men the lid began to yield.

BLAM

By this time the gipsies, seeing themselves covered by the Winchesters of Lord Godalming and Dr. Seward, made no further resistance.

The top of the box was thrown back.

KLOOF

I saw the Count lying within the box upon the scattered earth.

He was deathly pale, just like a waxen image, and the red eyes glared with the horrible vindictive look that I knew too well.

As I looked, the eyes saw the sinking sun, and the look of hate in them turned to triumph.

139

But, on the instant, came the sweep and flash of Jonathan's great knife.

HAUUUGGH!

SHLKK

Mr. Morris's bowie knife plunged into the heart.

GULGH!

SKTCH

AAARRGGHHH!

It was like a miracle; but before our very eyes, and almost in the drawing of a breath...

...the whole body crumbled into dust...

...and passed from our sight.

I shall be glad as long as I live that even in that moment of final dissolution, there was in the face a look of peace, such as I never could have imagined might have rested there.

Mr. Morris sunk to the ground.

QUINCEY!

I am only too **happy** to have been of any service!

Oh, God! It was worth **this** to die! **Look!**

AMEN!

AMEN!

The sun was now right down upon the mountain-top, and the red gleams fell upon my face, so that it was bathed in rosy light.

Now God be **thanked** that all has not been in **vain!**

See! The **snow** is not more **stainless** than her Forehead! The **curse** has passed **away!**

And, to our bitter grief, with a smile and in silence, he died, a gallant gentleman.

SEVEN YEARS AGO WE ALL WENT THROUGH THE FLAMES; AND THE HAPPINESS OF SOME OF US SINCE THEN IS, WE THINK, WELL WORTH THE PAIN WE ENDURED.

IT IS AN ADDED JOY TO MINA AND TO ME THAT OUR BOY'S BIRTHDAY IS THE SAME DAY AS THAT ON WHICH QUINCEY MORRIS DIED.

HIS MOTHER HOLDS THE SECRET BELIEF THAT SOME OF OUR BRAVE FRIEND'S SPIRIT HAS PASSED INTO HIM. HIS BUNDLE OF NAMES LINKS ALL OUR LITTLE BAND OF MEN TOGETHER; BUT WE CALL HIM QUINCEY.

WE CAN ALL LOOK BACK ON THE OLD TIME WITHOUT DESPAIR, FOR GODALMING AND SEWARD ARE BOTH HAPPILY MARRIED.

IN ALL THE MASS OF MATERIAL OF WHICH THE RECORD IS COMPOSED, THERE IS HARDLY ONE AUTHENTIC DOCUMENT; NOTHING BUT A MASS OF TYPE-WRITING, EXCEPT THE LATER NOTE-BOOKS OF MINA AND SEWARD AND MYSELF, AND VAN HELSING'S MEMORANDUM.

WE COULD HARDLY ASK ANYONE TO ACCEPT THESE AS PROOFS OF SO WILD A STORY.

WE WANT NO PROOFS; WE ASK NONE TO BELIEVE US!

THIS BOY WILL SOME DAY KNOW WHAT A BRAVE AND GALLANT WOMAN HIS MOTHER IS.

ALREADY HE KNOWS HER SWEETNESS AND LOVING CARE; LATER ON HE WILL UNDERSTAND HOW SOME MEN SO LOVED HER, THAT THEY DID DARE MUCH FOR HER SAKE.

143

In the summer of this year we made a journey to Transylvania, and went over the old ground which was, and is, to us so full of vivid and terrible memories.

It was almost impossible to believe that the things which we had seen with our own eyes and heard with our own ears were living truths. Every trace of all that had been was blotted out.

The castle stood as before, reared high above a waste of desolation.
— Jonathan Harker.